INDEPENDENCE

PETER REESE DOYLE

Drums of War

Providence
Foundation

Independence: Drums of War

Copyright © 1997 by Peter Reese Doyle.

Published by:
The Providence Foundation
P.O. Box 6759
Charlottesville, VA 22906
(804) 978-4535

Cover illustration and design:
Corky Nell

Illustrations:
page 6, Jason Brough
pages 54 and 89, Tanya Nevins

The Providence Foundation is a Christian educational organization whose purpose is to assist in the development of liberty, justice, and prosperity among the nations by teaching and equipping people in a Biblical philosophy of life. The Foundation teaches Christian principles of government and politics, economics and business, arts and sciences, education and family life, using historical models which illustrate their application.

Printed in the United States of America.

ISBN 1-887456-06-6

TABLE OF CONTENTS

With Thanks to God

for

SALLY ANN

*Who – in the Golden Glory of a late
Summer's Full Moon – stood with me beside
Bruton Parish Church, listened to my Plea,
and consented to become*

MY WIFE

THE DRUMS OF WAR

Virginia
April, 1775

Lord Dunmore stole the powder from the Public Magazine;
He sent by night a wagon filled with scarlet-clad marines;
He never dreamed his theft would cause Virginians near and
far
To march – at Patrick Henry's call – behind the Drums of
War!

For England's King had broken faith with every Colony,
Ignored their Constitutions and enforced the Tyranny
Great Britain's corrupt Parliament had recently proclaimed
Was theirs – by right! – to rule by ruthless Power in the
Name

Of Sovereign Force – unchecked by Law – of Might, by
Power of Arms!
And this had shocked the Colonists and caused their great
Alarm.
For now they feared that Parliament might close their
Churches down,
Establish State Religion, grind their Freedoms in the
Ground.

And now they knew they had to fight, to keep their Homes
and Land,
To fend off distant Government's insatiable Demand

Drums of War

To regulate their Daily Lives, corrupt their Children too,
Choke off Religious Liberty, and all Just Laws undo.

So when the noble Henry called, Virginians rallied round;
They marched toward Williamsburg and hoped that soon
  they'd hear the sound
That all was Well – that Government had heard the Warning
  Bells,
Would give them back their Powder – and their Liberties as
  well.

Chapter One

"THEY'RE STEALING OUR POWDER!"

The long wagon, axles greased to deaden the sound of the massive wheels, moved with unaccustomed silence through the cool darkness of the April night. Red-coated marines from the British warship Magdalen rode the wagon, muskets loaded and ready to fire. Captain Collins and the sergeant rode ahead, leading them carefully through the dark streets to the octagonal brick building called the Magazine. Here, a large amount of gunpowder was stored for the defense of the Colony of Virginia. Behind the wagon, two other mounted marines rode with muskets ready.

The marines were very alert, expecting trouble at any moment from the town's armed citizen-militia; they'd come to take gunpowder from the Magazine, and were prepared to fight their way out of town if they had to. They hoped they wouldn't have to.

An iron-clad wheel crushed a rock in the dirt road, making a horrible screech. "Quiet!" hissed the officer, head snapping back to glare at the driver. Periodically, the horses' hooves struck rocks with awful sounds, sounds the marines thought would surely wake the sleeping townspeople. But the houses they passed remained dark and quiet.

Nervously the marines watched these homes as they rode past with such agonizing slowness, wondering when they'd be spotted. But no one called out; no heads appeared in the windows; no lanterns were suddenly lit. The night watchman was nowhere to be seen.

"No one's heard us," the marine holding the reins whispered gratefully to the redcoat beside him on the wagon seat, who was barely visible in the darkness. This man, musket held upright between his knees, sighed with relief. Every minute he'd expected to hear a shout of alarm, followed by shots. *How can we fight our way through the whole town if the citizens discover us?* he asked himself.

"Those townspeople had better not hear us before we get the powder, or the captain will have us flogged!" he said to his companion.

"How can we get all those barrels out of the Magazine without **somebody** hearing us?" the driver whispered back. "The watchman tours the town all night long!"

"Yeah, but they know his routine. The sergeant said we'll get to the Powder Magazine while the watchman's on his way toward the College - that's at the west end of the town. He said we'll have plenty of time."

"He'd better be right!" the driver answered. "The lousy rebels are armed, every man of 'em, and we'll be right in the middle of town, completely surrounded. If anyone sounds the alarm before we finish, it'll be terrible! I don't like this at all!"

"Neither do I."

"Quiet!" the captain hissed again. Now, only the clopping of the horses hooves and the creaking of the wagon and the rumble of its wheels broke the quiet of the April night. But the driver thought that he could smell his own fear, and the fear of the other men in the wagon. He shivered.

"We're almost there, sir," the sergeant said quietly to Captain Collins, as the two men rode side-by-side, ahead of the wagon.

Out of the darkness ahead loomed the thick bulk of the brick Magazine and the high circular wall that surrounded it. Built in 1715 at the urgent request of Governor Alexander Spotswood, the Magazine had first stored the powder sent from the Tower of London for the protection of the colony during the French and Indian Wars of 1754 to 1763. At that time as much as sixty thousand pounds of gunpowder had been stored within the building. That was when the high circular wall was built around the Magazine to give this storehouse added protection for the munitions and weapons it contained. A guardhouse was also built just outside the wall, to house sentries to watch over the military stores within.

Captain Collins and the sergeant continued to walk their horses toward the Magazine. Thick sacks wrapped around the horses' hooves smothered most of the sounds of their passage. But the wagon still made noise: creaks and groans of straining wood, sharp crunches as the iron-clad wheels struck occasional stones in the street.

The marines, swaying with the wagon's motion, were on edge. Should the alarm be given now, they'd have a lot of houses to pass before they could get out of the town—houses with armed citizens who trained regularly to defend their

The Powder Magazine

homes. This wasn't England, and the marines knew it. These Americans were prepared to fight against invading soldiers and any government officers who threatened the safety of their wives and children!

Suddenly the wagon's wheel crushed another rock. The red-coated marines stiffened in alarm, hearts pounding, muskets raised and pointed outward toward the houses they passed. But no one challenged them. The town still slept. Releasing their breath, the invaders continued on their course toward the Magazine. Every step they took brought them deeper into the heart of the town - and danger.

The armed cavalcade finally reached their objective, the gate set in the north side of the wall around the Magazine. The Governor's messenger had told the Marines that there would be no guards in the guardhouse that night, and that the gate to the circular wall and the door of the Magazine itself would be left unlocked.

"Scout the area, Sergeant!" Captain Collins ordered as they approached the gate in the high wall that surrounded the strange-looking building. Obediently the sergeant wheeled his horse to the left and began to ride around the wall while the captain halted the wagon before the gate. In a few moments the sergeant completed his circle of the wall and rejoined the group of marines.

"All clear, sir!" he said.

"Excellent! Open the gate and get the powder!" Captain Collins ordered.

The sergeant leaped from the saddle with practiced ease, tied the horse's reins to the wagon, and ran to the gate. Pushing it open he went to the Magazine's door and entered, followed by a marine carrying an unlit lantern. Once inside, the lantern was lit. And there, inside the octagonally-shaped building, were the barrels of gunpowder, stacked neatly against the wall! Hanging the lantern on a hook by the door, the sergeant gave his orders crisply. The marines went swiftly to work removing the barrels and taking them to the waiting wagon.

Outside the circular wall, one marine, musket ready, took station facing the Duke of Gloucester Street. The two mounted men behind the wagon walked their horses around to the other side of the wall, and faced outward, alert for any danger. Captain Collins had prepared this operation with great care before leaving the ship, and each man knew exactly what to do.

Nervously the captain walked his horse slowly around the walls in a careful patrol, joining for a moment the sentry facing the center of town. "Hear anything?" he asked.

"No, sir," the sentry replied. In the darkness, the captain could make out the bulk of the man's body, but not his features.

Captain Collins began to think that they just might be able to remove the powder without alarming the town. Under the sergeant's direction the marines were filling the wagon with great speed, hauling barrel after barrel from the Magazine and loading these carefully into the wagon before returning for more.

"Those rebels will learn that they can't defy Great Britain!" Captain Collins said with grim satisfaction to the sentry standing guard. "Besides, our war with France is over; what do they need gunpowder for? **We're** protecting them!"

"Sir, do you really think the Americans will fight the King?" the sentry replied. None of the marines or officers on board the ship could believe that the colonists would be so stupid as to go to war against the might of the British Empire.

"No!" Captain Collins replied sardonically. "But they've got some hot-heads stirring them up, and they might make some foolish mistakes - unless we take away their gunpowder! They can't fight anybody without gunpowder!" he laughed quietly.

He looked through the darkness at the dark bulk of the Magazine and the blurred silhouettes of the men as they hurried to load the barrels in the wagon. "This is going like clockwork!" he exulted. "We'll have those rebels' powder, and they won't even know it's gone!" Smiling to himself with great satisfaction, he shifted in the saddle. He was beginning to relax. *These colonists are like helpless sheep!* he thought to himself.

The sound of the night watchman's pistol shattered the dark stillness of the night. Then the watchman started shouting, "They're stealing our powder!"

Windows flew open in the houses of the town, yells of alarm began to fill the air. Lanterns were lit in the windows. As the watchman reloaded his pistol he continued to shout, "They're stealing our powder! They're stealing our powder!"

"That's enough!" Captain Collins yelled with a curse, shocked and completely surprised! Drawing his pistol he wheeled his horse to face the dim form of the night watchman some forty yards away. "Let's go, Sergeant!" he called.

The marines tumbled out of the Magazine and jumped into the wagon. Slamming shut the heavy tail-gate, the sergeant raced toward his horse and leaped into the saddle. The big animal snorted and reared. The driver released the brake on the wagon, cracked his whip on the backs of the horses, and the animals broke into a run. The sudden motion tumbled two of the marines onto the barrels of powder. Captain Collins and the sergeant put their horses into a gallop and raced ahead of the running wagon. The marines inside the heavily laden wagon steadied themselves as best they could in the wildly rocking vehicle and aimed their muskets outward, ready to fire.

The two mounted marines galloped behind the racing wagon, muskets cocked and ready to shoot. Making a tremendous noise now, the deadly cavalcade roared through the dark streets of Williamsburg, prepared to fight through any band of citizens that dared to get in the way.

Lanterns were beginning to appear in windows on each side of the street through which the marines were racing.

Everywhere, men were shouting.

Would they make it to the boat that waited for them at the creek? The marines began to doubt that they would.

Chapter Two

"CALL OUT THE MILITIA!"

Andrew Hendricks woke at the sound of the watchman's pistol. Jumping out of bed, he groped his way through the dark to the partially opened window. Confused sounds came from the streets a block or so away as men called anxiously to each other, asking what had happened. Lanterns and candles began to appear in windows across the street. Somewhere in the city, a drum began to beat. Then another. And another. Dogs were barking furiously.

Turning from the window Andrew crossed the room to the table, groped for his flint, struck a light, and lit the candle. Hurriedly he pulled on shirt and trousers and shoes, grabbed the long rifle leaning in the corner with his powder horn and cartridge pouch, and rushed into the hall and down the stairs.

In the front hall below him his father was standing, rifle in hand. The lantern on the wall was lit, and in its flickering light Andrew saw his mother standing in her nightgown beside her husband. Shadows from the lantern light swirled around his mother and father as Andrew rushed down the stairs and joined them.

Andrew's sixteen-year old sister Laura rushed from her room, long reddish-brown hair falling to the shoulders of her white nightgown. "What's wrong, Father?" she cried, hazel eyes wide with surprise. Behind her hurried eleven-year old Rachel, brown eyes equally astonished at the sudden commotion and the increasing volume of noise in the streets.

"The alarm, Laura!" William Hendricks replied. "It's the alarm!" A tall man, lean, with dark hair, he'd already pulled on his brown trousers and dark hunting shirt, and was now loading his rifle with practiced ease. Andrew began to do the same. The girls crowded anxiously beside their mother.

Eight-year old Benjamin stumbled down the dark-paneled stairs after Andrew, rubbing sleep from his eyes. "What's happening?" he asked anxiously, rushing toward his mother and throwing his arms around her, eyes wide with fright. She held him close.

"I don't know, son," his father replied, smiling reassuringly and tousling his son's brown hair. "But Andrew and I will go see." He turned to his wife: "The two pistols are loaded, Carolyn. So are the rifles. Lock the door after we leave. Nelson and Nathan are next door; they'll watch out for you until we return. We'll be back as soon as we can."

His wife nodded confidently, smiled at her men as they left, then locked the door behind them. "Put on your robes, children," she said, "then come to the kitchen. We'll make some chocolate."

Benjamin brightened visibly at this and grinned at Rachel, who grinned back and rushed to her room for her robe.

Outside, Andrew and his father hurried through the dark streets toward the sound of the watchman's cries. Other men joined them as they began to approach the center of the commotion. Some of the men carried lanterns, others held torches, and Andrew and his father began to recognize people they knew. Drums were beating the alarm as the dark forms moved quickly through the darkness with a quietness strange for so many men. Whisperings of anxious conversations came to their ears, the scuffling of many hurrying feet scraped the ground, and the town's many dogs continued their frenzied barking.

Soon Andrew and his father reached a great crowd milling around in the wide field before the Magazine. Torches and lanterns cast weird shadows as agitated forms moved vigorously about in the seething mass of angered men. Their stomping feet kicked dust into the air, and Andrew coughed. Men were shouting out questions, yelling for answers, and brandishing muskets, rifles and torches in the confused and angry crowd. Gradually, the message filtered through the agitated mob: British soldiers had taken the gunpowder from the city's magazine!

"They stole our powder!" men shouted. The crowd roared in anger.

"Then let's take it back!" someone called.

Angry shouts of approval followed this reply. Andrew trembled at the animal emotion that swept the citizens. Two men beside him collided in the seething mass, and fell to the ground. His father grabbed Andrew by the shoulder and pulled him away.

"The Governor did it!" someone shouted. "The soldiers were using his wagon. He's trying to disarm us so we can't defend ourselves!"

The crowd roared again. The mood was ugly, violent. And most of the men were armed.

"Stick close, Andrew," William Hendricks said, his arm around his son's shoulders.

Men began to attempt to calm the crowd. "Let's wait until morning, and find out what really happened," a steady voice called out in a reasonable tone, trying to quiet the uproar and bring reason and wisdom to the milling crowd whose numbers were being swelled by a constant stream of new arrivals.

"We **know** what's happened!" a man shouted from the back of the mob. "The Governor's stolen our powder! What more do we need to know?"

"They're in a wagon, so they can't go that fast!" the night-watchman yelled. "We can catch them and take it back!"

A violent chorus of approval followed this cry. For several moments no one could be heard above the confused yelling. Then, several men began urging patience and caution. "We don't know enough!" someone yelled. "What can we lose by waiting for morning to get more information?"

"We can lose our powder!" a husky man shouted. Andrew could just make him out through the crowd: a stocky, red-faced young man with unkempt black hair.

"That's Jed Marks," Andrew's father said to his son. "He's a hot-head and a trouble-maker."

Marks was shouted down by men whom Andrew learned later were members of the House of Burgesses, Virginia's parliament. Gradually the mob quieted, as reasonable men sought to calm them. Groups began to break off from the crowd, some of the men going back to their homes, but others still clustered in heated discussion.

"Come with me, Andrew!" his father said quietly, as he moved through the shifting crowd. The boy followed his father, brushing shoulders with angered men, many of them armed as he was. Finally his father reached a group standing in front of the Market Square Tavern. "Come here, Hendricks," one of the men called. "We need your advice." Hendricks walked over to the group, Andrew close beside him. Soon the men were deep in discussion.

Around them the crowd seethed and thinned as men went home. Angered voices still rang out, but the passions of the mob had been calmed by reasonable men, and the situation was more stable now. Yet lanterns shone from every house, Andrew saw, and dogs were barking continuously.

In a few minutes Andrew's father and his friends had formulated their plans. One of the men summarized their decisions: "We'll notify the militia companies. We'll also notify the delegates of the House of Burgesses who've just gone home. And we'll send a messenger to Patrick Henry."

"He's the man to guide us now," Andrew's father agreed. He turned to his son: "Andrew, go tell Mr. Edwards what's going on. Tell him I'll see him in a little while. Then go back to the house. Tell your mother what's happened, and that there will be no action taken tonight. Everyone can go back to bed; I'll be home shortly."

"Yes, sir," Andrew replied, disappointed that he couldn't remain with the men. He turned obediently and headed back, his long rifle in his hand.

"Don't tell these plans to anyone else," his father cautioned.

"Yes, sir," Andrew answered. He hurried back toward the Edwards' house, which was right next to his own.

Nelson Edwards was a merchant in Williamsburg, the closest friend and business partner of Andrew's father. Edward's oldest son, Nathan, was fourteen, like Andrew, and was Andrew's best friend as well.

The two families had agreed that when the alarm was next sounded, Nelson and Nathan would stay home and watch the two houses while William and Andrew went to the gathering. "We can't leave both homes with no menfolks around," the two fathers had agreed. Andrew knew that Nathan and Mr. Edwards would be waiting eagerly for news about this latest commotion.

As he walked rapidly through the darkness, he saw that the crowds of men were continuing to disperse and return to their homes. Small groups still stood around talking, but their voices were lower now, calmer, as if they'd all agreed to wait for daylight and more information. Andrew crossed Nicholas Street, and hurried to the Edwards' home which was right beside his own.

As he approached the two-story house with its dormer windows, he saw that there were lanterns lit in the two front rooms downstairs. He raised the long brass knocker on the door, then let it fall. In a moment the door opened, and Mr. Edwards, rifle in hand, stood before him. Mrs. Edwards and her children stood in the hall.

"Come in, Andrew!" Nelson Edwards said, closing and locking the door after him. "Tell us what's going on." He and Nathan had both put on their trousers and long-sleeved shirts, and held rifles, powder horns and cartridge bags in their hands. Glass-covered candles on the walls shed their gentle light in the hall.

Andrew stood in their hall, a strong boy, taller than average for his fourteen years, with thick dark hair and brown eyes. He told the Edwards of the gathering at the Magazine. The family hung on his words with breathless interest as he related the message his father had sent him to deliver. Nathan, his dark hair still tousled from sleep, was wide-eyed with excitement. His sister Sarah, twelve, wearing her long blue robe, stood close beside her mother. The younger boys, Nelson, and Patrick, practically stood on Andrew's feet as they drank in his description of the mob around the Magazine.

When Andrew had delivered his father's message, Mr. Edwards nodded thoughtfully and leaned his rifle against the wall. His wife spoke then. "Come in the kitchen, Andrew," she smiled, "and join us for some chocolate."

Andrew hesitated. "I'd like that, ma'am, but I'd better go first and tell Mother what's happened. Then, if she doesn't mind, I'll be right back." He glanced at Sarah, who smiled shyly back.

"Certainly, Andrew," Mrs. Edwards said, "by all means go tell her your father's message. I'm sure she'll be anxious until she sees you. Then come back if you can."

"Can I go with him, Father?" Nathan asked, eyes gleaming; he was eager to get out of the house in this time of high excitement. Nathan was large for his age, tall as his father, with wavy brown hair, hazel eyes and a disarming smile.

"Yes, Nathan," his father smiled. "But leave your rifle here!"

"Yes, sir," Nathan said, as he rushed out the door behind Andrew and ran next door to Andrew's house. The two boys ran up the steps of the front porch and peered in a window, and Andrew tapped the glass with his knuckles. His sister Laura was the first to hear him. She came to the door and let the boys in. "We're all in the dining room," she said.

Rushing there the boys found Mrs. Hendricks with Rachel and Benjamin, drinking hot chocolate. Hurriedly Andrew told them what had happened, and that there was no danger threatening now. "Father will be home shortly," he concluded, "and Mrs. Edwards asked if I could come back with Nathan for some chocolate with them!"

Vastly relieved to hear that there was no present danger, his mother agreed at once. "Don't stay too late, though. Their children should go back to bed, and so should you!" She knew he wanted to tell the Edwards more about the night's excitement. She also knew how fond he was of Sarah.

"Yes, ma'am," he said gratefully, turning to leave. "But where's Nathan?" he asked in surprise.

Laura smiled, a twinkle in her hazel eyes, and told him, "He went to the kitchen with Rachel."

"She'd better not give him all those muffins!" Andrew said, alarmed. He had a terrible time keeping his friend away from Rachel's pies and muffins.

Just then Nathan rushed from the kitchen, followed by Rachel. "Gosh, those are great!" he told the young girl through a mouthful of food as he stuffed something quickly in his pocket. A guilty grin swept over his face when he saw the others were watching. Rachel laughed at his efforts to hide the muffins she'd just given him.

"Let's go before you can eat them all!" Andrew said sharply. Nathan winked at Rachel as the two boys rushed out the door, and she laughed back at him.

Chapter Three

"DOES THIS MEAN WAR?"

In the kitchen of the Edwards' home, Sarah and her mother were sitting at the table drinking hot chocolate from thick mugs while Nelson, Jr., eight, and Patrick, six, were playing with toy soldiers in the corner. The aroma from the steaming chocolate filled the room. Glass-covered candles were lit on two of the walls, as was a lantern on the dark wood table. The soft light flashed from the brass pots hanging by the fireplace, and was swallowed in the folds of the white curtains at the windows.

Sarah jumped up when her father and the boys entered the room. "I'll pour it, Mother!" she volunteered quickly. Hurrying to the fireplace she filled two mugs with steaming chocolate. Nathan followed her and picked up one of the mugs, while Mr. Edwards waved Andrew to a stool. Then Sarah brought the other mug and handed it to Andrew, smiling down at him as he took it from her hand.

"Thanks," he said gratefully, looking up at the lovely dark-haired girl in the long blue robe standing before him. Then, realizing that the whole family was watching, his tanned face began to redden.

But Sarah was laughing as she looked down at him. Andrew's dark hair, uncombed when he'd leaped out of bed, had been further tousled by his hat – now it was shooting from his head in all directions.

"My goodness, Andrew," she exclaimed, her deep blue eyes smiling down at him, " your hair's all standing up every which way! You must have been really scared by all that excitement tonight!"

"I wasn't scared of anything," he replied matter-of-factly, his face still red. "I just didn't have a lot of time to primp and get pretty when Father and I rushed with our guns to answer the alarm."

They all laughed at that. Then Mr. Edwards looked at his two young sons. "Nelson and Patrick, back to bed with you! Everything's all right now. Mother will tuck you in."

Reluctantly the two boys got up and headed for the stairs, followed by their mother. "I'll read you a story first," she told them, "since you're all awake right now." This brought smiles to their faces; they waved good night to Andrew as they left the room, and he waved back at them.

"Tell me more about the gathering, Andrew," Mr. Edwards said sitting down on the bench against the back wall. Sarah sat down beside her father, rested her head against his shoulder, and looked at Andrew expectantly. Her father put his arm around her and listened intently as the boy told his tale. Andrew, very conscious of Sarah's gaze, tried hard to look at Mr. Edwards and not at her.

"There were crowds of men there, sir," he replied. "A lot of them were shouting. Some of them had lanterns and torches, and many had muskets or rifles. Men were yelling that the British soldiers had stolen the powder from the Magazine, and that they'd used the Governor's wagon to take it away."

Mr. Edwards shook his head, his bright blue eyes deeply troubled. "If that's true, it was a foolish thing for the Governor to do! That will inflame the whole colony. Even reasonable men will fear British tyranny now. If the Governor takes away the powder we've stored for our protection, it means the British government wants us to be defenseless against them."

"I heard Father tell the men tonight that this may be a good thing after all," Andrew said. "He said that the British government intends to take away our self-government and enslave us, and this action tonight will make our people understand that. Lots of people just can't bring themselves to believe what the British plan to do to the colonies, and Father said that this would help wake some of them up to the truth. The other men agreed with him, sir."

"I think your father's right, Andrew," Mr. Edwards said, regarding the boy more somberly. "But it's tragic that things have come to this. It didn't have to happen." He sighed.

Andrew looked at his father's best friend and business partner. Nelson Edwards was stocky, not fat but strong, with a genial face that smiled easily. His hair was thick and dark, almost black. Andrew's father had told him how wise Nelson Edwards was. "He's got great courage, too," his father had told him often. "He can fight with his fists, and he can shoot. I'm glad he's my partner – and our neighbor!"

Edwards spoke again, almost to himself. "The American colonists have tried everything to avoid this. We've sent humble letters to the British government, begging them to let us maintain the constitutional rights of Englishmen. But they wouldn't listen." He shook his head sadly.

Then, remembering his guest, he looked up. "More chocolate, Andrew? Sarah, I bet he'll drink more - if *you* pour it for him!"

Andrew's face flamed red at this – was Mr. Edwards teasing him? Sarah jumped up with a laugh, took Andrew's mug from him, and filled it again from the pot by the fire. Mr. Edwards never teased Andrew about Sarah, and this was a complete surprise to the boy. As if he'd gone too far, Edwards wiped the broad grin from his face and began to question Andrew more about the men who'd gathered around the Magazine, asking whom he'd recognized.

Just then they all heard a knock on the front door. "I believe that might be your father, Andrew," Mr. Edwards said as he rose. Nathan went with him to let in Mr. Hendricks. Andrew and Sarah looked at each other.

"I made a custard pie," she said. "Would you like some?"

"Sure," he said, relaxing now that the others had left the room. She hopped up and went to the cupboard, took out the pie, cut a large piece and brought it to him on a pewter plate.

"Do you think we'll have a war?" she asked, pulling over a stool and sitting in front of him as he began to eat.

"My father thinks so," Andrew said through a mouthful. "Gosh, Sarah, this is great pie!"

She smiled. Then, seeing he'd soon eat it all, she jumped up and crossed the room to the cupboard. Cutting another slice just as big as the first, she brought this in her hand, put it on his plate, and sat down again before him. She leaned forward, hands clasped around her knees, pleased at his obvious enjoyment of the pie.

He smiled his thanks. "You sure can cook! I hope your father doesn't get mad at me when he sees his pie's gone!"

"I'll make him another," she laughed. Andrew loved her pies, and she always found ways to give him some.

Then the smile faded from her lovely face. "So your father thinks there'll be fighting against the English soldiers?" she asked, deep blue eyes somber, long dark hair falling down to her shoulders. She hugged her knees as she sat on the stool before him and looked up earnestly into his dark eyes.

"He does. So do his friends. They say that the British Parliament is bent on taking away the liberties of all the American Colonies. They think the English believe they've got to prove that they're boss. After they conquer all of Massachusetts, they'll do the same to the other colonies."

His face was grave. Unlike many of the boys his age who welcomed the idea of war, Andrew had learned from his father that war was a dreadful thing, with fearful consequences and immeasurable damage, destruction, suffering, and death.

"Would you and Nathan have to go and fight the English soldiers?" she asked solemnly, her eyes troubled at the thought.

"I don't know," he replied. "We'll do what our fathers tell us. If the British try to make us slaves, we'll have to fight them.

Or if they invade our houses and put soldiers to live with my family, or with you and your family, like they do in other parts of their empire, I'd fight 'em then," he said with deep conviction as he looked back at the gentle girl before him. A chill came over his heart at the thought of the horrors of British soldiers being put to live in Sarah's home, and in his own.

For a long moment she looked at him without speaking.

Suddenly her father and Mr. Hendricks entered the room, followed by Nathan. Andrew and Sarah stood up respectfully.

"Time to go home, Andrew!" Mr. Hendricks said with a smile. "We've got work for you and Nathan to do tomorrow, and you'd better get all the rest that you can!"

"What kind of work, Father?" Andrew asked eagerly, as he saw the excitement in Nathan's eyes - obviously, he knew already!

"You're going to be couriers for us," his father replied. "We're sending messengers to all the militia companies in the different counties, telling them about the theft of our gunpowder. You and Nathan will ride out in the morning!"

"Gosh!" Andrew said, excitement beaming from his dark eyes, long face breaking into a huge smile. He grinned his thanks to Sarah as he handed her the empty pewter plate.

"Sarah, did you give that young scoundrel my custard pie?" her father cried in alarm as he stared at the bare plate in her hands.

"He was hungry, Father," she replied, blushing. "Wouldn't you want me to feed a guest if he's hungry? You know what the Bible says!"

Mr. Edwards laughed and hugged her shoulder. "How can I deny that?" he asked. Then he shook Andrew's hand in his strong grip. "Thanks for bringing us the news, Andrew!" He was very fond of this boy, and everyone in both families knew it.

"Yes, sir," Andrew replied, turning and following his father to the door.

"I'll take him home before he eats your breakfast, Nelson," William Hendricks laughed.

As they walked the few steps to their home, Mr. Hendricks told his son more about the reasons for the decisions he and his friends had made. "This is a serious development, Andrew - that the Royal Governor would steal the Colony's gunpowder! We've bought that powder at our own expense; it's not his to take! We don't know what he plans to do next, and that's why we want to alert the Colony's militia companies!"

"But the British have already made it against the law for the colonies to import gunpowder," Andrew replied. "If they steal what we have, we won't be able to stop anything their government wants to do to us, will we?"

"That's right, Andrew. We won't. This looks like a concerted effort to disarm us. To make us slaves. That's why this is so serious. Whenever citizens are unable to defend themselves against the people in power over them, they lose their liberties–

that's one of the lessons of history. That's what we're facing now."

"And Nathan and I will be riding together?" Andrew asked, pleased at the job they'd been given.

"Yes. You two will ride out with Matthew Anderson toward Richmond, taking letters for the patriots' committees. Then you'll separate; Anderson will head for the western counties, while you and Nathan turn south and circle back to Williamsburg, delivering letters to our contact men. You can spend the night at William Johnson's farm, and return the next day. Other men will be riding out also. We want to get this news to the captains of militia companies, to the chairmen of our committees of correspondence, and to other patriots as well."

They climbed the steps to their front porch. William Hendricks clapped his son on the shoulder: "So, to bed with both of us! We've got work to do tomorrow!"

Chapter Four

CITIZENS IN ARMS!

But Andrew and Nathan did not ride out with Matthew Anderson the next morning. Before their families had finished breakfast, a courier rushed to their homes with letters from the patriot leaders. Nelson Edwards received his first, read it, excused himself and with Nathan by his side went immediately next door to confer with William Hendricks. Somewhere in the town, men were beating drums.

"Militia companies are already marching, Father!" Nathan said excitedly, as they hurried across the yard to the Hendricks' home.

"You're right, Nathan," Nelson Edwards replied, shaking his head. "Things have become very serious. But the more militia we have with us, the more seriously Governor Dunmore will have to consider our demand that he return the gunpowder he stole from the Magazine!"

They went up the steps of the Hendricks' back porch and knocked on the kitchen door. William Hendricks opened the door at once. "Come in!" he said, his face somber. "Plans have changed, it seems, Nelson."

"Only temporarily, I believe," Edwards replied. "Our leaders plan to confront the Governor this morning, and they want us to wait until after that meeting before we issue an alarm to the militia in the other counties."

"That makes good sense," William Hendricks agreed, as he led them to the dining room and waved them to chairs.

The two men sat in the dining room, and Nathan and Andrew joined them around the dark cherry table. From the kitchen came the pleasant aroma of cooking bacon. Together the men spread out the messages they'd received, and compared their contents.

"Peyton Randolph is anxious that we calm the townspeople and avoid a mob getting out of hand," Hendricks said quietly, looking up from the letter, dark eyes somber.

"I agree with him completely," Edwards replied, "but I also agree with those men who insist that we can't let the Governor get away with stealing our powder!"

"You're right about that!" Hendricks said, his face grave. "I'm afraid that Peyton doesn't appreciate that point; he's such a reasonable man himself that he thinks others are reasonable also. In politics – and in war – that can be a serious mistake! Have you heard when they plan to meet with the Governor?"

"No, I haven't. Let's go about our business until we get word of the meeting." He grinned at Nathan: "This means, young man, that you can work all morning for us before you tear off on a wild adventure carrying messages for the Committee of Correspondence."

"Yes, sir!" Nathan said, "That's fine!" His face beamed with pleasure at the adventure before him and Andrew that day.

"Also," Edwards continued, with a straight face, as he rose and turned to leave, "with Andrew out of town for a couple of days, maybe my daughter will cook a pie for **me**!"

Hendricks laughed out loud at that as Andrew's face flamed red. Nathan grinned at his friend's embarrassment, waved, and followed his father home.

But there was not much work accomplished at Edwards' and Hendricks' office that morning. The small building behind the Hendricks' home was the scene where more messengers arrived during the morning. At nine o'clock, another rider galloped through the open gate and drew rein at the door of the office. Nelson Edwards walked out the door to receive the letter the man handed him. Then the messenger wheeled his big bay horse and galloped away.

Frowning with concentration, Nelson opened the letter and began to read as he stepped through the door and into the office. William Hendricks looked up from his desk. "What news now, Nelson?" he asked, leaning back in his chair. His coat was hanging from the chair in which he sat, and he'd opened the collar of his white shirt.

Edwards scanned the letter, then looked at his partner, his face grave. "They want us, William. I've told Nathan to stay home and guard the house, and keep the children inside. There are too many men around town today!"

"I'm ready," Hendricks said, rising and putting on his coat. "My family's staying inside also."

The men walked out of the building and headed toward Hendricks' house. They had just reached the steps to the back porch when Laura Hendricks came out of the door, breathless with excitement. She wore a light brown dress with a long white apron, and her eyes shone as she spoke.

"Father," she said pleadingly, "may I go and visit Mary on Duke of Gloucester Street? We'd be able to see everything from her house!" Mary was a friend of Laura's whose home looked out onto the town's main street.

"No indeed, Laura!" her father replied at once. "Why do you think the Edwards are staying inside? Women don't belong on the streets when the town's filled with troops of men! Especially not on Duke of Gloucester Street – that's where all the companies are gathering! You stay inside with the family."

Andrew came out on the porch behind her, and Hendricks spoke to him. "Andrew, keep the rifles handy, and guard these folks for me!"

"Yes, sir," Andrew replied. His father had already told him of the crowds of militiamen that had gathered in town, and of the need to keep the women and children in their homes.

"All right, Father," Laura said, trying to hide her disappointment. She walked back into the house, followed by Andrew.

Hendricks and Edwards walked around the house and out to the gate. At once the drums were louder, more stirring. Directly in front of the house trooped another militia company behind the electrifying beating of three drummers. The marching men, clad in long hunting shirts, fringed trousers, long rifles sloped over their shoulders, passed purposefully by, singing a rousing song about liberty. In the distance, other drums and fifes could be heard as more groups of militia converged on the center of the town. Dust swirled around the feet of the marching men, and dogs ran alongside, barking furiously.

"This looks ominous, Nelson," William Hendricks said, his face grave, as the two men followed the militia company toward the center of town. "I hope that our leaders will be able to keep the men from doing something rash that would provoke the Governor to take action. Governor Dunmore is not a patient man."

"He's not," Nelson Edwards answered quietly. "Nor does he appreciate being confronted like this. We'd better pray that the militia can be kept in order, and that no hot-heads provoke the British guards."

Inside the Hendricks' house, Andrew and Laura and Benjamin pressed their faces against the front windows as yet another company of armed men strode vigorously by, singing songs of war. Across the street, two small boys had climbed the branches of a tree so they could watch the militia pass. The marching men wore tough canvass shirts and wide-brimmed hats. Tomahawks, knives, and cartridge boxes hung from their belts. The long muskets angled over their shoulders in martial array. They looked fierce and very capable.

"Boy!" Andrew exclaimed, eyes wide with excitement, "the Governor had better give back that powder before our men blow him out of his Palace!"

"How many men do you think there are?" Rachel asked, awed.

"Hundreds, I bet!" he replied. "I think they're coming from all over to help us get our powder back!"

Three long hours passed before Andrew heard his father's steps on the front porch. He and his sisters rushed toward the door just as William Hendricks let himself in. He took off his dark tricorn hat, then handed Andrew a thick package of letters bound with a dark cord.

"Here are the messages, Andrew," he said. "But there may be more, so you and Nathan will wait until tomorrow morning to leave. Matthew Anderson will go with you part of the way. He'll have a package to take to the western counties while you and Nathan circle to the south and deliver these. You'll be back the day after."

"Yes, sir!" Andrew said, ecstatic that he and Nathan would be entrusted with such an important mission for the Patriot cause.

The day passed in a blur after that. Andrew and Nathan worked in their fathers' warehouse with the hired hands while their fathers visited with other Patriots in town.

Later that afternoon, when William Hendricks came home, Laura rushed up to him and asked anxiously, "Father, Andrew and Nathan won't be in any danger, will they?"

"No, Laura, they won't," he said, hanging up his coat and hat on the rack by the door. "They're just taking messages to a few of the local patriot leaders. They'll be back the day after tomorrow!" He smiled to reassure her.

"But will the Governor try to stop them?" she asked, not satisfied.

"No!" her father laughed as he put his arm around her shoulders and smiled down at her. "He's too busy fortifying

his palace against all the militia in town!" Then his smile
faded. "Trouble is, he thinks that **we** might attack him. We
won't, I'm sure – but he **thinks** that we will. Such a man is
dangerous, unless we can persuade him that we only want our
powder back."

That night William Hendricks informed his family that they
would go to bed earlier then usual. "Andrew and Nathan have
a long ride ahead of them tomorrow," he reminded them, "so
let's make sure they get a good rest." He gathered them around
the table and opened the big family Bible to the Book of Psalms.
The candles on the walls shed a gentle light in the dark-paneled
room. Andrew saw Rachel's brown eyes looking at him with
great solemnity. Laura looked real serious too, he noted, and
so did his mother.

"Read Psalm thirty-four, William," his wife asked. "It's a
wonderful encouragement for times like these."

"Certainly, Carolyn," he replied. He turned to the Psalm,
and began to read. The powerful Word of God spoke to them
all, from Father to little Benjamin. They prayed after this, then
went to bed. Tomorrow would be a long day for Andrew and
Nathan.

The next morning brought more messengers on galloping
horses. Shortly after seven o'clock, Hendricks told his son to
gather his equipment for the trip; then he followed Andrew
upstairs to his room. Pride shone from the father's eyes as he
looked at his nearly-grown son, clad in a long fringed tan
buckskin hunting shirt, with knife and tomahawk in their
sheaths on his belt. Andrew wore brown trousers and long
moccasins, and was just slinging his powder horn and bullet

pouch over his shoulder. His brown eyes gleamed with unconcealed excitement as his long face broke into a smile.

"Thanks for letting me go on this mission, Father," he said gratefully.

Hendricks smiled at the boy's pleasure. "We need your help, Andrew. You're almost grown, you can do the work of a man already, and you can handle your weapons. And you've got good sense." He paused, then grinned and concluded, "And you've also got Matthew Anderson to keep you out of trouble!"

They both laughed at this. "Not all the way," Andrew reminded his father as they headed down the stairs. "He'll leave us and head for Richmond!"

"True, so use your good sense, and get back here as soon as you can tomorrow. Johnson will be glad to put you up for the night – I've given you a letter for him also. But you can tell him that I think we can still ship his peas and pork and butter to Philadelphia safely; it's Boston that the British have blockaded, and that's far to the north. They're not stopping shipments to Philadelphia."

This prompted Andrew to ask a question that had been bothering him for some time, ever since the port of Boston had been blockaded and closed by the British fleet. "Father, if the British declare war against us, they'll blockade all our ports. That will endanger your shipping business, won't it?"

"That will endanger everything, Andrew, every business that we have in the Colonies. But it can't be helped; if we don't defend our families and our property, we'll have no business left." He clapped his son on the shoulder as they reached the front hall. "Go in the kitchen and tell your mother good-by. She's packed some food for you. And remember, she'll be worried until you return."

"Yes, sir," Andrew replied, leaning his long rifle in the corner. "I'll remind her that Nathan and I have gone with Matthew lots of times, and that this is no different."

"Fine," his father said. "And you have. But with all the noise and confusion and alarms now, she's worried. Mothers can't help worrying about their children, you know. Besides, things are different, now, with war looming. So make her laugh if you can."

"Yes, sir," Andrew said with a grin, "I can always do that!"

Hendricks watched his sturdy son step into the kitchen. In a moment, he heard his wife and daughter laughing at something Andrew had told them. Hendricks smiled.

Chapter Five

THE RIDE TO MORGAN'S TAVERN

Andrew and Nathan were standing beside their horses, packs already behind their saddles, long rifles in their hands, when Matthew Anderson rode up and dismounted in front of the Hendricks' house. A lean and wiry man, not tall, not as tall as Nathan, in fact, Anderson was a noted woodsman and Indian fighter. His broad, tanned face beamed at the two boys affectionately. He'd often taken them hunting with him, had taught them much about woodcraft and wilderness fighting, and had also trained them to throw their knives and tomahawks with great skill. They were thrilled that they were going to ride with him and carry the alarm to patriots who lived outside of Williamsburg.

"Hi, boys!" he said as he dismounted, and tied the reins of his dappled gray to the rail. "Ready to ride?"

"Yes, sir!" they replied eagerly.

"Got your rifles, I see," Anderson noted with satisfaction. "Think you know how to shoot those big guns?" he asked with a twinkle in his gray eyes. His weathered, brown face looked solemn as he appeared to question their capacity to shoot.

"We can try, sir!" Nathan laughed.

This was a question Anderson asked them frequently, a standing joke between them, in fact. Actually, both boys were deadly shots with the long rifles, and he'd praised them often. Further, he'd taught them to shoot and reload while running - just like the Indian fighters in the western counties. He was proud of them and their skill, and had told them he'd be happy to have them with him any time he got in a fight.

Just then William Hendricks and Nelson Edwards came out of Andrew's house. "Here are the letters, Matthew," Hendricks said, descending the steps and handing the woodsman a thick package wrapped in oilskin. "The names are on 'em. You know the men already."

"Reckon I do," Anderson acknowledged as he scanned the list of names written on the outside of the package. The leaders of the patriot cause had kept in touch with each other with every new development in the dispute between the Colonies and Great Britain, and Anderson had taken many such messages to these same men.

"Those are to the militia captains and the committee chairmen, Matthew. The boys are carrying letters, too, to some of the men between here and Richmond. They'll ride with you part way, then turn on the road to Morgan's Tavern."

"Glad to have them with me," Anderson replied. He grinned at the boys, then stuffed the letters in the pack behind his saddle.

"Nathan," Sarah called from the front of her house next door. "You and Andrew come here for a minute."

The two boys walked over to the Edwards' porch. Sarah, in a light blue dress with white apron, her long dark hair framing her face, stepped from the porch and handed each a package wrapped in thick paper. "Here, take this for your trip." Her eyes were troubled; she'd already told her brother that she feared for the two boys as they prepared to go on this journey.

"Thanks," Nathan said, taking the package in one hand and hugging her around her shoulders with his other.

Andrew took the package she handed him and thanked her. Then he was silent, not knowing what to say. Sarah was obviously worried. He couldn't understand why women sometimes got sad when men went on adventures like this. His sister, Laura, was worried too, and had pestered her father with questions about Andrew's mission, wondering if he'd be in danger. It amazed him that his father was always so patient to listen to the fears of Laura and her mother, and usually was able to comfort them.

Sarah realized that she'd been looking at Andrew a long time and hadn't said anything. She flushed. "Be careful," she told him finally, dropping her eyes.

"Sure I will!" he replied, with a grin. "What's this?"

"You'll see," she said, glancing up at him again. "You can open it when you eat lunch." Then, as he continued to grin at her, she smiled shyly back.

"Let's go!" Anderson called.

The boys turned and hastened to the horses. Andrew was riding his father's big brown mare; Nathan rode a gray. The sun was already warm, and flies were bothering the horses. The big animals were fidgeting, stamping their feet and swishing their tails. A rider galloped past, raising a trail of dust.

William Hendricks looked at the two boys fondly. Each wore a long hunting shirt, with their brown trousers stuffed in high-topped moccasins. Each had a tomahawk and long knife in his belt. Wide-brimmed hats topped their heads. They were almost fully grown, trained to work and to fight, and Hendricks knew they were ready to face whatever dangers came their way. William Hendricks was proud of his son, as he knew Nelson Edwards was of Nathan.

"Let's ask the Lord to protect these men on this trip," William Hendricks said. They bowed their heads, and he prayed for their safety. When he'd finished, Nelson Edwards prayed too. "And, O God, please protect the Colonies from the British armies!"

They all said "Amen" to that.

"Let's ride," Matthew Anderson said casually, stepping into the saddle. Andrew and Nathan slung their long rifles across their backs by the leather straps, and swung into their saddles. Waving good-by to their fathers, they turned the horses and began to trot toward the road to Richmond. Their mothers and their brothers and sisters stood in the doors of their homes and waved; the boys waved back.

In a few moments the three horsemen approached the College where the road divided: to the left was Jamestown, to the right, Richmond. Between the fork of the road and directly ahead of them were the magnificent brick buildings of the College of William and Mary. The riders turned their mounts to the right.

"Did you hear what the Governor's saying?" Anderson asked the two boys as they put their horses into a trot.

"Yes, sir," Andrew replied. "A messenger told us that the Governor said he was surprised that the people were upset about the powder, that he'd only taken it because he'd heard that some powder was stolen in a nearby county, and that he'd return it in half an hour whenever it was needed."

"That's a false rumor," Anderson said grimly. "The Governor invented it, in fact. No powder was stolen in another county. The only powder that was stolen was ours, and he stole it! But the latest thing he's said is that if we did anything to the marines who took the powder from the Magazine, he'd order the British forces to destroy the city with their cannons!"

"What?" the boys gasped. They looked at the grim-faced woodsman in utter surprise.

"That's right," Anderson repeated. "He threatened to destroy Williamsburg."

"What are the leaders in the House of Burgesses saying?" Andrew asked.

"Peyton Randolph and some of the others are saying that we should calm down, that the issue is settled, that nothing more should be done," Anderson replied. "Randolph's a great man, but in this matter some of us think he's too cautious. We think that if we don't stand up to this action of the Governor's, there'll be no stopping the British. We've got to stand up now and get our powder back, or they'll never believe that we'll defend ourselves! They'll take our guns away next!"

This was a shock to the boys. The government take away peoples' guns? They looked earnestly at the woodsman to see if he was serious.

He was very serious. "That's what they'll do," he repeated. Anderson added thoughtfully: "That's the lesson of life, boys. If people think you won't fight back, they'll walk all over you. It's the folks who are ready and willing and able to defend themselves who most often don't have to. That's why your fathers have taught you both to fight. That's why we can't ever let people take away our weapons and the means to defend ourselves and our families!"

Then, almost to himself, he said quietly: "But now I think we won't be able to avoid a war with Great Britain. I think they'll force us to it."

The three rode past a few more houses, and then they were out of town, following the rough road through fields and then through woods. Riders passed them occasionally from the other away. The three overtook some supply wagons; folks waved as they rode by, and the three waved back. Gradually the traffic slowed. The road wound through deep woods now, what folks called 'wilderness', good hunting country, and Anderson said he wished they had time to look for deer.

They ran the horses periodically, then slowed them to a walk to conserve their strength. Around noon they stopped at a creek to let the animals drink. Then they rode over to the edge of a clearing, tied the horses to trees, and found a shady spot under the broad branches. Sitting down in the shade of the tall trees, they took out their food: thick slices of bread and meat, some nuts, berries, and water from their canteens proved a satisfying meal. When they'd finished, the boys took out the packages Sarah had given them and opened them.

"Pie!" Andrew exclaimed with pleasure, as he unwrapped his. She'd given Nathan the same. They each had two thick pieces, and both boys offered a piece to Anderson.

"Thanks, boys, but I'll decline, and smoke instead." Taking out his pipe he packed it with tobacco and lit up. The three lounged comfortably for a few minutes while the boys ate the fresh pieces of pie Sarah had made for them. Birds were singing in the woods behind them, and in this pleasant interlude the boys almost forgot the serious mission they were on. But after a while, Anderson stood and stretched. He grinned at the boys and kicked at Andrew's foot. "Time to go!" At once their minds returned to the task at hand, and the boys rose.

The three untied their horses, mounted, and headed again toward Richmond along the narrow road that wound through the forest. Anderson was always a rich fund of information, and the boys questioned him about every possible subject as they rode. Finally they came to a fork in the road that branched off to the left. Anderson called a halt.

"Here's where we split up," he said with a smile on his tanned face, leaning across the pommel of his saddle, looking at them with a penetrating glance of his gray eyes. "You boys be careful. Keep your eyes and ears open."

"Yes, sir," they replied, wishing they could go on with him to the western counties.

"Where's your first stop?" the woodsman asked thoughtfully.

"Morgan's Tavern," Andrew replied. "We'll give Morgan a batch of letters to give to some militiamen."

Anderson's weathered face was grave, and he didn't say anything for a moment. Andrew had a sudden thought that the woodsman was worried about Morgan.

Finally, Anderson replied. "Just be careful, like I said; keep your eyes and ears open," he repeated.

Then he straightened in his saddle, grinned at the two, waved his hand and put the big gray into a lope toward Richmond. Feeling somewhat alone without the confident woodsman's company, Andrew and Nathan turned their horses onto the road that forked to the left, and put the animals into a run. Trees overshadowed the rough passage at this point, and they passed through deep shadows thrown across the uneven road.

Andrew had a strange feeling that Anderson's warning to keep their eyes and ears open was really meant to alert them when they got to Morgan's Tavern. Didn't the woodsman trust Morgan? If not, why hadn't he expressed his suspicions to their fathers in Williamsburg? As they rode through the dark forest, Andrew pondered Anderson's hesitation in speaking about Morgan. Maybe, he thought to himself, the woodsman had suspicions, but not enough evidence to justify expressing them. Andrew felt a strange sense of foreboding about Morgan.

Now they rode into patches of light that fell through breaks in the tall trees. The road climbed a gentle hill, turning to the south as it did so. Birds were calling and chattering to either side of the road, and suddenly a deer ran across their path! The horses snorted and pulled up suddenly.

"No time for hunting now!" Nathan said ruefully, putting his mount in motion again. "It'd take us too long to skin him."

Andrew agreed reluctantly.

"Wonder how many men are riding out from Williamsburg with these messages?" Nathan asked. "Father said that men were writing all night long to get these letters ready."

"Must be a lot of 'em," Andrew said. "There's lots of militiamen to alert. Since the convention in Richmond last month, when Patrick Henry made his resolution, all the counties are supposed to form troops. That's what made the Governor mad, they say, and that's why he decided to take the powder - so we wouldn't ever be able to oppose the British soldiers."

For another hour they rode along the rough narrow way that wound through the tall trees. Then the road began to climb, and suddenly it led them into a clearing. Small cultivated fields stretched to both sides, and before them was a weathered two-story wooden structure once painted gray, with decrepit, unpainted outbuildings behind it. At the rail in front of the large building, under the shade of a giant oak's wide-spreading branches, a half-dozen horses were tied. Trash littered the grounds around the buildings.

"That's Morgan's Tavern," Andrew said.

"Wonder who those horses belong to?" Nathan asked curiously, as they approached the rail. "Two of 'em have been ridden hard!" The boys took note of the pair of big steeds that stood with heads down and bodies covered with sweat.

"Those animals are worn out," Nathan observed, wondering what urgent business had made the animals' riders push them so hard.

"One of them's from town," Andrew said suddenly. "I saw that big black in front of the Governor's Palace, yesterday maybe."

"Let's be careful, like Mr. Anderson said," Nathan reminded his friend as the two dismounted and tied their horses to the rail. Slipping their long rifles from their shoulders, they mounted the wide wooden steps and entered the entrance hall of the tavern. From within came the sound of men's voices.

Chapter Six

THE FIGHT AT THE TAVERN

Inside the door Andrew and Nathan stopped and stood a moment, letting their eyes adjust to the darkened interior. Before them, the long hall led to the back of the house. To the left and right, doors opened into rooms with high-backed wooden booths and tables. The ceiling was low, the floors dirty, and the whole place smelled of stale beer and cooking grease. The boys could hear men talking in the room to their left. Andrew threw a quick glance at Nathan, then walked warily toward the door. Nathan was right behind him.

"Come in, boys," a hearty voice called as the two stepped through the door and paused. Across the darkened room, against the wall, three men sat at a table, drinking from tall mugs. "Set, and I'll be with you in a minute," the voice called again.

The speaker was a large man whose huge body almost overwhelmed the chair in which he sat. Thick wrists and big hands jutted from the loose sleeves of his dirty blue shirt. His right hand dwarfed a thick mug of beer. Massive shoulders sloped up to the man's badly battered ears, and it seemed as if he had no neck at all. Graying-black hair topped a large rounded face.

"Thanks," Andrew replied. He chose a booth to the right, and the two walked over, leaned their long rifles against the dark-paneled wall, and sat down on opposite sides of the rough-hewn wooden table. Andrew pulled the package of letters from his belt, and placed it on the scarred wooden surface in front of him. After the fresh air of the outdoors, the tavern seemed stifling and oppressive. And dark. *And dangerous, somehow,* Andrew thought.

"That must be Morgan," Nathan said quietly, looking across the room at the massive hulk who'd greeted them.

"That's him," Andrew replied, just as quietly. "I met him last year when Father took me through here. But who are his friends?"

They glanced cautiously at the two men talking with Morgan. Both were dressed for riding, and both leaned across the table toward the innkeeper in earnest conversation. One was small, slender, clothed in a black shirt and trousers. *He almost looks like a clerk,* Andrew thought to himself. The other man wore a fringed buckskin shirt and pants and was huge, bigger even than Morgan, but without any fat. One hand dwarfed a large tankard, the other rested on the curved handle of a long pistol hanging in a leather holster from his belt.

"They've switched to French," Andrew said quietly to Nathan. "They were speaking English when we were on the porch."

"I noticed that," Nathan said, with a frown on his face. "We'd better not let them see us looking; they don't want us to understand what they're saying."

"Shhh!" Andrew whispered, "I think we'll be able to hear them!"

Both boys relaxed in the dark-paneled booth, beginning to enjoy the rest from their long ride, in spite of the oppressive atmosphere of the tavern. The room's only light came from two small windows in the front of the building and from one in the side wall, to the right of the table where the three men sat. Gradually, as the boys remained silent, Morgan and his companions seemed to forget that they were there; their voices became louder. Morgan was speaking now, still in French. Obviously, it didn't occur to the men that the boys might understand that language.

"Tell the Governor I'll let him know what those rebels in Williamsburg plan to do," Morgan said. "They'll contact me like they always do - they think I'm still on their side! - and when they do, I'll pass the message on to him right away. If they're sending out messengers like you say, I should be getting letters today. I'll copy them, and Johnny will deliver them to the Governor in Williamsburg tonight."

"Fine," the smaller man said with a crooked smile, relaxing and leaning back in his chair. He took a long drink of beer from his mug.

His huge companion looked suddenly at the boys. His dirty hunting shirt swelled with the muscles of his large frame; dark trousers were stuffed in muddy boots. The man exuded danger.

Andrew and Nathan began to wish they'd stayed outside the tavern.

"Who are those boys?" the big man asked Morgan in a gravelly voice, still speaking French, still staring at Andrew and Nathan.

The innkeeper squinted in concentration as he looked across the dark room at Andrew and Nathan. "One of them seems familiar-like, but I can't rec'lect his name. I think he's from town."

"They wouldn't be carrying messages, would they?" the big man asked, a glint of interest lighting his pale gray eyes. A coarse, rough-looking brute, his face showed scars from what must have been some vicious fights. He continued to stare menacingly across the room at Andrew and Nathan.

"I doubt it," Morgan said, "they wouldn't send boys. There'll be a man coming soon." He took a long pull from his mug and wiped his mouth on his dirty sleeve. "Maybe I'd better serve them so's they don't get suspicious." Heaving his bulk out of the chair he shambled heavily across the room and came to a stop close beside the boys' table. He stretched his face into a hearty smile as he looked down at Andrew and Nathan. "What can I get you boys?" he asked - in English.

They both asked for a tankard of apple cider.

"Just a minute, boys," Morgan said, "I'll be right back." The innkeeper turned and lumbered out of the room. Andrew and Nathan talked quietly with each other, trying to calm their increasing nervousness. Nathan glanced over at the two seated men, then looked back quickly. The big man was still staring at them. When Andrew saw the muscles of Nathan's face tighten, he dropped his hand to the tomahawk in his belt.

In a moment Morgan was back, returning with two tall pewter tankards which he set down on the table. Nathan asked the price, and when Morgan named it, paid with coins. Morgan scooped these up quickly in his thick hand and stuffed them in his pocket as both boys took long drinks of the cool cider.

But the tavern keeper's eye had fallen on the packet of letters lying on the table in front of Andrew. Raising thick bushy eyebrows in surprise, he asked suddenly, "Those letters wouldn't be for me, would they now, boys? My name's Morgan." His thick red face beamed down at them in a friendly way, dark eyes squinting out of folds of fat. His face smiled, but his eyes were cold, Andrew noted.

"No, sir," Andrew said quickly, covering the packet with his hand. Now he wished that he'd kept these on the bench beside him.

"What you doing with 'em here?" Morgan asked suspiciously, thick face frowning. His geniality was gone completely. Now he seemed dangerous.

"I'm carrying these for my father," Andrew said quickly. His muscles tensed.

"Zed," Morgan called, without turning around, still staring menacingly at Andrew.

Across the room, the big man in buckskins scraped back his chair quickly, then moved with cat-like grace to stand beside Morgan, directly before Andrew. The smaller man in black slid quietly to Morgan's left, blocking Nathan. Now the boys were trapped in the booth by the three threatening men.

"Let's see those letters, boy!" Zed said in a rough voice, pale eyes glaring ominously, huge hands dangling at his sides.

"No, sir," Andrew said, "they belong to my father." Zed stood directly to his left. Andrew tightened his grip on the tall pewter tankard.

With surprising speed Zed grabbed Andrew by the shirt front and hauled him with great force out of the booth. But Andrew had been ready, legs tensed on the floor. Uncoiling his lean frame with all the strength of his legs, he shot from the booth and brought the pewter tankard around in a vicious arc, smashing the rim into Zed's face at the bridge of the man's long nose.

With a yell of pain Zed stumbled back, drenched with cider, blood spouting from his nose, hands flying to his face. Following the staggering man with great speed, Andrew swung the heavy pewter tankard again, smashing it across the side of the bully's head. Zed crashed to the floor.

Dropping the tankard Andrew leaped across the fallen hulk, spun around, and with a speed Morgan and the smaller man never expected, faced them with his long knife in one hand and raised tomahawk in the other – he was ready to throw!

"Whoa, boy!" Morgan said, as the two startled men backed hastily away at this surprising violence from the boy they thought they could bully, "Easy, now! Don't throw that thing!" Morgan's red-rimmed eyes were wide, his heavy jowls shook with fright at the deadly tomahawk poised above Andrew's head. One wrong move and he knew the boy would throw.

The smaller man's eyes were white with fear as he stared at the boy's lightning reactions and the raised tomahawk. He licked his lips nervously as he continued to back away. "Careful, boy," he said, "you're in trouble now!"

Suddenly the loud snap of a rifle being cocked jerked the men's attention back to Nathan. Concentrating only on the danger from Andrew's knife and raised tomahawk, they hadn't heard Nathan rise and pick up his rifle. Now their shocked eyes saw that he was standing beside the edge of the bench, long rifle held waist-high and aimed directly toward them.

"Hey, boy! Put that gun down!" Morgan said hastily, his thick face shaking with fear.

"Yes, sir," Nathan replied, "when we leave here I will. That man had no reason to yank my friend like that, Mr. Morgan!"

"No, boy, he sure didn't!" Morgan agreed hastily. "He sure didn't!" The steady glint in Nathan's darkened eyes scared him as much as the rifle aimed at his quivering middle. *This boy's dangerous!* Morgan thought in alarm.

"Zed'll kill you for this!" the small man said viciously, turning back to Andrew and smiling maliciously. "When he comes to he'll track you down and kill you!"

"Then my father will see that he hangs pretty high from the gallows in Williamsburg," Andrew said quietly. His heart was thudding from the sudden action – and fear.

As Nathan covered the two with his rifle, Andrew stepped swiftly to the table, put his knife and tomahawk back in their sheaths, and stuffed the pack of letters in his belt. Then he picked up his rifle. Cocking the hammer he turned the deadly

Andrew and Nathan carefully retreat from the tavern.

barrel toward Morgan and the man in black. Both boys could feel their hearts pounding in their chests – but both held their rifles with rock-like steadiness on the two men.

Zed, lying on the floor, was absolutely still, clearly unconscious. His face was covered with blood, his breathing ragged.

"You boys get out of here!" Morgan said hastily, anger beginning to show in his thick red face. He'd been bested by two boys and it was beginning to gall him. He was convinced that those letters were for him. "Leave those letters; they're for me. I know it! – and get out."

"The letters are ours, Mr. Morgan," Nathan said evenly, rifle very steady. The muzzle of that boy's rifle seemed to grow bigger and bigger the more Morgan looked at it, and the innkeeper began to quake.

"Give us room to leave, Mr. Morgan," Nathan said.

Morgan and the smaller man backed hastily toward their table. Andrew and Nathan moved warily toward the door, rifles trained on their foes. Suddenly Nathan stepped across to the fallen man on the floor, stooped, and yanked the pistol out of Zed's holster. Stuffing this in his belt, he trained his rifle on Morgan and his companion once more, and backed to the door where Andrew was waiting. For a moment the two boys stood there, rifles held waist-high.

"Untie the horses while I watch 'em," Andrew said, his rifle pointing directly at the space between the two men.

Morgan and the man in black were not about to interfere. They realized now that these boys could probably shoot rifles as well as wield knives and tomahawks – and pewter tankards!

Still backing toward their table, they bumped clumsily into their chairs. Morgan tripped and fell on the floor with a tremendous crash. Cursing, he lifted himself laboriously and fell into his chair. The other man sat down also, swearing under his breath, livid with rage and afraid of what the boys might do.

Nathan turned without a word and ran through the door.

"We won't bother you, boy," Morgan said huskily to Andrew, who stood rock-still, gun still aimed. "Just git!" With a shaking hand he picked up the tall tankard and took a long drink.

Andrew didn't say anything. He stood waiting, watching them, rifle steady.

Then Nathan called from the front yard. "I've got the horses! Let's go!"

Andrew backed through the door and into the hall, his rifle still trained on the men. He called to Nathan: "Aim for the window, and I'll cover the door."

"I'll leave this pistol in the yard, Mr. Morgan," Nathan called.

"You'd better, boy, or you'll go to jail!" Morgan yelled back, angered again, his blood boiling now.

"Better for stealing than for killing a man," Andrew said evenly. His voice was calm – but his heart was racing, and every sense was alert.

Then he turned and ran through the tavern door and across the porch, leaped down the steps, vaulted into the saddle and grabbed the reins Nathan tossed him. Whirling his big steed, Nathan hurled the heavy pistol across the yard, far from the tavern. The two kicked their horses into a gallop, and they thundered out of the yard and down the road. The horses galloped side by side, racing for the safety of the woods ahead.

Chapter Seven

THE RACE TO
JOHNSON'S FARM

Both boys looked back when they'd covered some fifty yards from the tavern on their galloping steeds. "They're not going to bother us!" Nathan called over the pounding noise of the horses' hooves. They grinned at each other with obvious relief. But they held their reins in their left hands and their rifles ready in their right, resting across their saddles.

"That was a great idea taking that pistol away!" Andrew said.

"I didn't want them to shoot us in the back!"

Galloping furiously side-by-side down the road they began to feel safer with each yard of distance gained from the tavern and the dangerous men inside.

"Those men are spies for the Governor!" Nathan said as their racing horses pounded along the rough dirt road and under the cover of the tall trees.

"If we hadn't known French, we wouldn't have understood them!" Andrew called back. "We wouldn't have known that they were spies, and I'd have given those letters to them! And they'd have sent them to the Governor this evening!"

"Who's next on the list?" Nathan asked, as they rounded a bend in the road and passed out of sight of Morgan's tavern. The horses were running easily, hooves flying across the dirt road, taking them farther and farther from the sinister group behind them. Patches of sunlight falling through the branches of the tall trees splashed on the road before them.

"William Johnson. He's got a farm some six miles from here. I'll recognize his place."

"We'd better tell him about Morgan and the Governor's spies!" Nathan said. "And give him the letter you were going to hand Morgan."

After a while they slowed their horses to give them a rest. But both boys kept looking behind them for signs of pursuit. There were none as yet, but they kept watching repeatedly. And they kept their rifles in hand, resting across the pommels of their saddles.

"That was great work with that tankard!" Nathan said admiringly, grinning at his friend. "He thought you were a boy he could throw around the room!"

"I caught him by surprise; that's how I got him!" Andrew admitted. "Gosh, he's huge! And did you see those scars on his face?"

"Yeah. We'd better watch out for him. But I think that if we pass the word to the patriots, they'll take care of him for us."

"I sure hope you're right!" Andrew said. He looked at his friend with a worried frown. "We've got to get back to

Williamsburg with this news about Morgan, that he's a spy for the Governor! The patriots don't know that."

"First we've got to tell Johnson," Nathan agreed.

The sounds of their horses' hooves were strangely muffled in this section of the road; the ground seemed damp. Then they crossed a shallow creek, splashing through the water and up a steep bank. Here they rested their horses for a few moments, looking back for signs of pursuit. They saw no one. Here also light splashed through the trees and fell in uneven patches on the ground.

"Wonder what those men will do when Zed comes to?" Andrew asked his friend.

"I don't know," Nathan replied. "But it's a good thing we didn't plan to go back to Williamsburg by the tavern!"

"It sure is!" Andrew agreed. "Morgan mentioned someone named 'Johnny' - guess that's a man who works for him. There were six horses in front of the tavern."

"And there were more in the fenced yard behind," Andrew said. "Wonder how many men he's got?"

"Do you think the Governor's got other men looking to intercept the letters from Williamsburg?" Nathan asked.

"I wouldn't be surprised," Andrew replied. "Lots of people don't want to offend England in any way. They'll do anything to keep peace."

"What kind of peace is it when the government steals your gunpowder, closes your ports and sends soldiers to occupy your cities?'' Nathan asked. "That's what's happening to Boston! And that's what will happen to us, our fathers say, if we don't defend ourselves!''

Deeply troubled at the danger they'd just encountered, and the realization that the Governor had spies in the patriot ranks, the boys rode on, looking back repeatedly to make sure they weren't being pursued.

Andrew thought they'd never find Johnson's farm, but at last they did. To the right of the road appeared a rough-hewn split rail fence, behind which was a cultivated field. Behind that were more tall trees. Soon the two boys came to a rough road leading to the right. Turning off the pike, the boys walked their horses toward Johnson's house, passing between trees whose shade covered the road with a blanket of shadow. Andrew warned Nathan what was coming.

"Get ready for a wrestling match! Caleb and Joshua will challenge you! They're bigger than I am, and can't get used to the fact that I can beat 'em, so they keep trying. They're strong, and they're fast, but they don't know our tricks!'' he grinned.

"Did you tell them we've got real Indians teaching us every week?'' Nathan laughed.

"I did not," Andrew said with a laugh. "I told them I was just born with great natural skill! They can't stand it!''

Andrew and Nathan were unusually fortunate to have the friendship of Moses and Abraham, two Christian Indians on scholarships at the College of William and Mary. These Indians taught them wrestling – at which American Indians excelled.

The Hendricks and the Edwards had repaid this kindness by treating Moses and Abraham to meals in their homes. This wrestling training gave Andrew and Nathan a terrific edge in their friendly bouts with other boys in Williamsburg, and was responsible for Andrew's victories over Caleb and Joshua.

Caleb was the first to spot them as they rode under the tall trees to the house. Tall, broad-shouldered, with a shock of wild yellow hair, he yelled out a greeting, put down the ax he was wielding, and called his family. Soon Andrew and Nathan were sitting in the large kitchen, mouths watering at the smell of newly baked bread, telling their story to the friendly family. Caleb and Joshua were the oldest, sixteen and fifteen, respectively. Mary was fourteen and Susan was ten.

The Johnsons were sobered by the news of the Governor's action in stealing the Colony's gunpowder. "I'll get this information to the right men immediately!" Mr. Johnson told them. "Tell your fathers we're grateful, and that we'll be ready for anything the leaders in Williamsburg suggest."

Johnson was a lean wiry man with thick yellow hair and a red face that never seemed to tan. His wife was short and plump, as dark as he was blond. She invited Andrew and Nathan to eat and spend the night with them. "It's too far to go back tonight," she said. "Besides, our children haven't had company for a while. William, you can get out your fiddle after supper and we can sing!"

"I think the boys want Andrew to give them a lesson in wrestling first, Martha," her husband said with a straight face.

"Father!" Caleb protested. "**We're** going to give **him** a lesson. He was lucky last time, but we're ready for him now!"

"Well, finish packing those barrels first," their father told them with a laugh. "Then see how much you can teach Andrew." He looked over at Nathan Edwards. "Looks like Nathan might be pretty good too," he said.

"We'll give him a lesson as well!" Joshua said with a grin. The boys laughed together. Andrew winked at Nathan.

For another hour, Andrew and Nathan helped Caleb and Joshua pack the barrels which Johnson would take to Williamsburg and ship to Philadelphia on Hendricks' and Edwards' schooners. William Johnson and other farmers in the area regularly shipped their peas, pork and butter to the northern colonies, so Andrew's and Nathan's fathers knew many of them.

Then, when they'd finished their chores, Andrew and Nathan followed the Johnson boys into the field for their match.

At supper that night, Susan looked up from her plate with a wide grin and asked her brothers, "Who won the wrestling match?"

Caleb and Joshua hesitated, their faces turning red. Andrew and Nathan said nothing. Mary answered her little sister's question: "I know! Andrew and Nathan did!"

"Well, they were lucky again!" Caleb admitted ruefully. He laughed, "But we'll be ready for them next time!"

"We sure will!" Joshua agreed. "They won't catch us with those tricks again!"

When they'd finished their supper, the girls helped their mom to clean up while the boys followed Mr. Johnson toward the barn to see to the horses. Then they all gathered in the big kitchen, laughing and talking while Mr. Johnson brought out his fiddle and began to tune it. In a few minutes, he began to play. Soon they were all singing together. Half an hour later he put the instrument aside, went over to the desk, and picked up the big family Bible. Returning to his chair, he opened the Bible and began to read from the book of Nehemiah.

The family and their guests listened as he read of how Nehemiah inspired and guided the demoralized Hebrews who were being intimidated by the nations around them.

"They were surrounded by hostile peoples," Mr. Johnson explained, "enemy nations who were determined to prevent them from rebuilding the walls of Jerusalem."

"Why didn't they want the Hebrews to rebuild the walls of their city?" Caleb asked.

"Because," his father replied, "without walls, the city was helpless. Their enemies could march in and capture the people, make slaves of them all, and steal their property whenever they wished to do so. But with walls around the city, the Hebrews could defend themselves and their families from enemy invasion. And they could practice the religion of the Covenant that the Lord had given them."

"That's just what the British want to do by stealing our gunpowder, Mr. Johnson," Andrew said. "Unless we can defend ourselves against their armies, they can tax away almost all that we have whenever they want."

"You're right, Andrew!" Mr. Johnson replied soberly. "That's the lesson of history! And there's something else. They can also prevent us from worshipping God as we believe He commands us to do. In Canada, the British Government has already made an agreement with the Roman Catholic Church, making that religion the official church of the colony. Protestants there may loose their religious freedom. Imagine - the very reason so many Englishmen left England to come to the New World was to practice the religion the Bible describes. Now, this liberty may be taken from them."

He pointed his finger to the Bible on his lap. "And this, in effect, is the same problem that the Hebrews faced under Nehemiah – their enemies would make them slaves, and prevent them from worshipping and serving God as the Bible commands them to do. That's why Nehemiah's task was so important. He had to organize and lead the Israelites to defend themselves first, so that they could then enjoy political liberty to obey God as the Bible describes."

"That's why the mission Andrew and Nathan are on is so important also," Mrs. Johnson said thoughtfully, looking seriously at the two boys. "By taking these letters from Williamsburg to the patriot committees, you two are helping Virginians in the struggle to keep our freedoms."

Andrew and Nathan were complimented by this remark. But all of the children were sobered to see the real connection between the tyranny that threatened the ancient Hebrews under Nehemiah, and the tyranny that threatened their families now from the policies of the British Government.

Mr. Johnson looked again at the pages before him, and began to read. The family listened to the story of how the Hebrews had determined to defend themselves. They'd built the walls of defense even as they'd held their weapons ready to fight off an enemy attack.

"That's what God has charged men to do," Mr. Johnson said soberly, closing the Bible. "Men have got to be ready to defend their wives, children and property from those who would harm and rob them. Evil and violent men exist in every age, and decent men must be willing and able – and that means, armed and trained – to fight them!"

His eyes were serious as he looked at his sons, Caleb and Joshua, and then over to Andrew and Nathan. "That's why it's so important for you boys to keep up your wrestling, and your shooting, so you can defend your families. We may have to do this sooner than we think!"

He led the family in prayer, then, as they sat around the big table in the kitchen, giving each, even the youngest, an opportunity to pray. Then it was time for bed, and they all turned in. Andrew and Nathan slept in the room with Caleb and Joshua.

Worn out from the long ride, from the fight in the tavern, from the work and then from wrestling with Caleb and Joshua, Andrew and Nathan slept well!

They rose early the next day, and prepared to leave right after breakfast. "The boys and I will get these letters to the right men!" Johnson told them as they said good-by. "I sent my hired hand over to the militia captain yesterday afternoon with the news about Morgan and the Governor's spies. Our men will check on them today." He chuckled grimly, then added, "I don't think they'll bother you for awhile, but watch out for them when you get back to Williamsburg."

Leaving the friendly family, Andrew and Nathan rode through the morning, stopping several times to deliver their letters and ask directions to the next man on their list. At Smith's Ordinary, a tavern smaller than Morgan's but a lot neater, the boys were given a huge meal for lunch.

"Eat up, boys!" Mrs. Smith insisted as she brought each of them a gigantic slice of pie after the meal. "You've had a long trip, and we don't want you to look wretched and starved when you get home. Your mother would never forgive me, Andrew!" she laughed. Then she handed him another package, wrapped in brown paper and tied with a strong string. "Here are the letters she let me read; tell her I loved them. I'm lending her some from my grandparents that I think she'll enjoy. We were so surprised to learn that we both have Huguenot ancestry!"

Then she looked reprovingly at her older sons. "But I'm afraid I haven't been able to interest these boys in learning French, as you and Nathan have done."

"Well, it sure came in handy yesterday, Mrs. Johnson," Andrew said fervently. "If we hadn't known French, we wouldn't have understood what Morgan and those men were saying. I'd have given him those letters, and he'd have sent them to the Governor!"

Then they said good-by and left the house. Stuffed to the gills with all the food she'd fed them, the two staggered to their horses, mounted somehow, and rode away – with extra pieces of pie in the packs behind their saddles.

Chapter Eight

THE LONG RIDE HOME

"Gosh, what a meal!" Andrew said as they rode their horses through a shallow creek that crossed the road. "Every time she offered me more food, I found that I couldn't say 'No!' "

"Wouldn't have made any difference if you had!" Nathan replied, "She wouldn't have heard you. No wonder those boys of theirs are so big! I'm glad that *they* didn't challenge us to wrestle!"

"So am I!" Andrew agreed. "Mr. Smith said he'd pass the word about Morgan and his men. I don't think we have to worry about them coming up behind us!" Andrew found that it was hard to get Morgan and his men out of his mind.

"No," Nathan said thoughtfully, "but we'll have to watch out for them in Williamsburg. You especially, Andrew, 'cause you really laid that big guy low! He'll never forget."

Nathan thought about this for a minute, then added: "But with the patriots so organized now, Mr. Smith said that all our militia will be watching out for those men, so we'll have lots of help if we need it."

Both boys rode with their long rifles in hand, resting across the saddles before them. They were very alert, looking frequently behind them as they covered the rest of their journey.

Twice more they halted at farms to deliver their remaining letters. At each place, they told about Morgan and the two men from the Governor's office. "We'll watch out for them!" the patriots assured them.

The ride home seemed to take forever. They were tired now, and ready to finish their journey. The sun was low in the sky, and its rays through the trees cast long shadows across the road.

"What's going on in Williamsburg, do you think?" Nathan asked his friend. "I sure wish we were there!" He shifted in the saddle to ease his tired muscles.

"So do I!" Andrew replied. "I bet there are a lot more militia companies now. When they hear that Governor Dunmore says he'll blow down the town with his cannon, they'll sure be mad!"

"Gosh, they could be fighting already!" Nathan exclaimed.

"I don't think so," Andrew said. "We've got too many men for the Governor to fight right now. But some people are worried that he'll escape to the British ships and bring back marines."

Nathan thought about this a minute. "Well, there aren't many British ships in Virginia waters, so there couldn't be many marines. And there's lots of our militia. I think you're right. I think the Governor won't dare to fight until he gets more men."

Andrew pondered his friend's words. Then his expression became even more serious. "We've got to remember, though, that the British are sending fourteen regiments of soldiers to

Boston. They're probably planning to send some here as well, so the Governor might have a lot more men soon."

Both boys were sobered by the thought of British armies moving into their city. They'd all heard how brutally the English were treating the people of Scotland. They'd heard of the horrible things that happened to women and children when Scottish homes were forced to house the British soldiers. Fervently they prayed that would never happen in Virginia, or in any of the other American Colonies. Periodically they put their horses into a lope, anxious to complete their mission. The long day wore on as they continued wearily toward home.

Tired, hungry, and thirsty, the boys rode into Williamsburg after dark. They noted with relief that the town seemed to be quiet. Lights shone from the windows of homes they passed, but there were no signs or sounds of fighting. They passed the College of William and Mary, and headed down Duke of Gloucester Street at a trot. Passing Bruton Parish Church on their left, they rode past the Palace Green and saw to their right the wide field with the Powder Magazine looming up in the dark. They rode on, turned to their right, and crossed Francis Street, heading home.

As they approached their homes, Nathan asked his friend, "Wonder what happened here while we were gone?"

"We'll soon find out," Andrew replied. "See you tomorrow!"

Nathan waved and dismounted. Andrew rode on past Nathan's house, then dismounted in front of his own. His body was stiff from the long day in the saddle, and he led the brown mare to the barn some distance behind his house. Here he stripped off the saddle and rubbed down the animal, who seemed as glad as he to be home! Andrew poured feed into the trough, gave her water, and left the barn.

Lights shone from the downstairs windows of the house as Andrew trudged wearily to the back door. None of his family had seen him ride up, so when he stepped up on the porch and opened the door he surprised them all.

The first to see him was Laura. She shrieked, "Here's Andrew!" and ran and threw her arms around his neck. He hugged her and grinned as the others gathered around.

Soon Andrew – at his father's insistence – was lounging in his father's chair in the kitchen, gladly telling of his adventures on the road. He was surrounded by his family, all except for Benjamin, who was already asleep. The lanterns and candles shed their glow over the cozy room, flashing light off the pots, glasses and china. The warm smell of hot chocolate cheered his spirits as he ate the cold meat pie his mother cut for him, and he thought how happy he was to be back. Morgan, Zed and the man in black seemed far away, too far away to threaten him now.

His mother's gray eyes had shown alarm when he'd told of the fight with Zed in the tavern. But she didn't say anything; he knew from experience that she'd ask him when Rachel wasn't present. "I'm mighty proud of you, Andrew," was all she said.

"So am I!" his father said emphatically. "That was a real trap you and Nathan were in, boxed in the booth by those big men. When did you know you'd have to fight?"

"When Morgan called Zed. Morgan was all smiles at first. But when he saw those letters, he knew they were for him, and he called Zed over. That man Zed is dangerous, Father – I was scared!" The muscles of Andrew's face tightened as he re-membered the sinister man. "I knew we couldn't get out of there with the letters if we didn't fight. So while he was walking over, I thought about what I would do. But I didn't let on."

"Well, you were smart about it, hitting him unexpectedly like that. But remember, you're more important to us than any letters. Don't ever fight when you don't have to." Hendricks had always told his son this.

"Yes, sir. And I didn't want to fight. But when he grabbed me like that, I just had to hit him and get away. Then Nathan made Morgan and the other man back off. I sure felt good when I heard him cock his rifle! Those men were really scared then, because he was ready to shoot!"

"Would you have thrown that tomahawk, Andrew?" Laura asked, her eyes wide with alarm as she remembered his story.

Andrew's face was grave, his eyes troubled. But when he spoke his voice was firm. "Yes, I would have thrown it. If they'd attacked me or Nathan, I would have had to throw it. Things had gone too far by then; those men would have hurt us if we hadn't been able to fight." He looked back to his father who was leaning against the door, holding a mug of hot chocolate in his hand, regarding him with thoughtful eyes. "Father, if you and Matthew hadn't taught me how to use weapons, it would have been bad."

"Perhaps," his father replied; "But perhaps not. They'd have thrown you on the floor, taken the letters, and kicked you and Nathan out of the tavern. They wouldn't really have hurt you. But you wouldn't have been able to defend yourself, or help the patriot cause like you have!" He straightened, finished the chocolate, and looked at his son with a level gaze. "You've done a fine job, son!"

Andrew's face flushed with his father's words of praise.

"And he's also traveled a long way these past two days!" his mother declared, standing up. "It's time for all of us to go to bed!"

As they prepared to go to their rooms for the night, William Hendricks spoke quietly to Andrew: "We'll meet Nathan and his father in the morning, then let you two tell this story to some of the patriot leaders. They've got to know that Morgan is a spy for the Governor – this is a complete surprise!"

"Yes, sir," Andrew replied.

"I'm proud of you, son!" his father said again.

"Thank you, sir," Andrew replied with a grateful grin. "I'm thankful that the Lord got us safely out of that tavern!"

"So am I!"

Andrew turned and began to climb the narrow staircase. He moved with great weariness, barely able to put one foot in front of the other, and never remembered taking off his clothes and falling into bed.

Chapter Nine

WAR IN MASSACHUSETTS!

Later the next morning, Andrew and Nathan rode to the landing where one of their fathers' schooners was docked. In their leather saddlebags were letters for the boat to deliver to Philadelphia.

"How many men were we talking to this morning?" Andrew asked as they rode, remembering the awe-inspiring gathering of leading figures he'd met in the Edwards' home. The men had been keenly interested in the boys' tale about Morgan and his two companions.

"More than a dozen, I think, but I was too scared to count!" Nathan replied.

"They sure asked us a lot of questions," Andrew said thoughtfully. "But they listened, too."

"They did," Nathan agreed. "And they said that Morgan had been loyal up to now, but that he owed the Governor money, and was about to be summoned to court."

"I guess that's what changed his loyalty, all right. It sure shows what can happen when a man gets in debt. Father tells us often that the Bible warns us not to get in debt, 'cause it makes us slaves to the people we owe. That's what happened to Morgan, I guess. Those men said that Morgan had been a real patriot before, and that's why it was such a shock to them to learn that he planned to copy the letters and send them to the Governor."

Andrew ducked as his horse passed under the low branches of a tree. Nathan ducked too. The road was rough, filled with old potholes from previous winter rains, hard and difficult in spots for the heavy wagons that brought the freight to and from the landing that served as a small port for the town of Williamsburg. The forest hemmed in the road on both sides.

Arriving at the river, the two dismounted, tied their horses to nearby trees, left their rifles, and walked over to the schooner. The sleek vessel was tied up alongside the small dock. On the deck of the craft they saw the powerful figure of John Turnbull, the schooner's captain, supervising the loading of barrels from a wagon.

"Hello," Turnbull called, when he saw the boys approach, "wait a minute 'til I load this cargo, then we'll talk."

Turnbull, a large dark-haired man, was a great friend, and had taken the boys to Philadelphia and Baltimore on previous voyages. He'd also taught them to sail the schooner. Hendricks and Edwards wanted their older sons to learn their business thoroughly, and the shipping of agricultural goods from Virginia to the northern states was a major part of the two families' enterprises.

The boys stayed out of the way while the loading progressed. Two sailors and two Negroes who'd driven the wagon from town were loading barrels onto the schooner with quiet efficiency. Soon the job was completed, and when the wagon turned and headed for town, Turnbull called the boys on board.

The Morning Star was not a large schooner, displacing only twelve tons, but its regular trips from Virginia to Philadelphia were part of the vital commerce that was helping to make the various colonies more helpful to each other and a bit less dependent on England. Consistent with its policy for all of its overseas colonies, the English government passed laws that prevented them from developing self-sufficient industry and commerce. Nevertheless, the ingenious Americans had turned their energies into new directions, and already iron products, furniture, and other manufactured goods from the northern colonies were freeing those in the south from having to buy these things from England. And the agricultural products from Virginia saved the northerners from buying these from the mother country, at excessively expensive prices. This small schooner was doing its part to further unite the colonies.

Andrew and Nathan passed across the plank gangway from the dock and stepped onto the deck of the vessel. Gray, with white trim, the sleek schooner was the joy of its master. "Going to sail with me to Philadelphia?" Turnbull asked as he led them to the stern. Here he leaned against the rail, took out his pipe, and built a smoke.

"No, sir," Nathan laughed, "not this time. We've got some letters for you to take to the Committees of Correspondence in Philadelphia."

"Let me have them," Turnbull said, taking the bulky package from Nathan's hand. "How much money do you think the patriots are spending for all these letters?" he asked with a quizzical look as he puffed his pipe. Paper was very expensive, and he knew that a lot of it was passing between the various Committees of Correspondence in the American colonies.

"I'm afraid to ask," Andrew answered. "Father says that they're spending a fortune on paper, but he says it's worth it. If the patriots didn't keep up with each other like this, the British could conquer one colony at a time, and the other American colonies wouldn't know what was happening until it was too late!"

"You're right about that!" Turnbull agreed. "Creating these committees in every colony was a stroke of genius! Sam Adams of Massachusetts thought of it back in '72, and it's been the major instrument in forging colonial unity ever since because we can tell the other colonies what the British are doing here in Virginia, and they can tell us what's happening with them. That way, the actions of the British Parliament and their armies and fleet are known to us all."

Turnbull's stocky frame filled the rough canvass trousers and shirt that he wore. Again the boys noticed the strength of the master's arms, the bulge of muscles that had hauled lines and steered vessels for years. Turnbull turned the package over in his hand, scanning the names with shrewd blue eyes under bushy eyebrows. "Reckon these tell about Governor Dunmore's stealing our powder," he surmised.

"Yes, sir," Nathan replied. "And about the messages to the militia companies in the other counties."

Flocks of gulls circled overhead, a sight which never ceased to fascinate the boys. They'd marveled at the birds' ability to spot small fish in the water, then dive for these with sudden plunges.

Turnbull reached in his shirt and pulled out a long thick envelope. "Give this to your fathers," he said, handing it to Andrew. "Don't lose it!"

"What's it about?" Andrew asked, eyes eager with curiosity. "Can you tell us?"

"I sure can, but don't say a word to anyone but your fathers. The British did the same thing in Massachusetts that Governor Dunmore did here: they sent troops to take the patriots' gunpowder and destroy their canons. But they didn't get away with it! In fact, they almost didn't get back! If General Gage hadn't sent about a thousand men to the rescue, the soldiers would have had to surrender to the Massachusetts militia!"

The boys were astounded at this news. "How'd that happen?" Nathan asked.

"General Gage sent hundreds of soldiers to capture the powder the militia had stored in Lexington. On the way there, a fight broke out – no one in Philadelphia yet knows how. But the British redcoats suddenly fired on our militiamen. That brought out dozens of militia companies from all the neighboring towns, and when they learned that Americans had been killed by British soldiers, they attacked the redcoats and harassed them all the way back to Boston! They fought all day long. The British lost almost three hundred killed and wounded!"

"Then it's war!" Nathan said solemnly, his mouth suddenly dry with the realization that hostilities had already begun.

"Looks like it," Turnbull replied. "I just got this news in a dispatch from a schooner three hours ago. We've got to be careful – you know how rumors run wild! But your fathers and the other men have got to know this."

"Are you in any danger from British ships then?" Andrew asked.

"Not that I know of, Andrew. They don't steal crewmen from boats this small. And no war's been declared, except against Boston. So our coastal trade is still going on, and I expect it will continue."

He looked soberly at the two boys. "Tell your fathers I'm waiting for the other wagons. Then I'll sail in the morning, like they told me to do. But if they want to send more messages, get them to me tonight."

"Yes, sir," the boys replied. They said good-by and left the ship.

As they rode home, the boys discussed the ominous news from the north. "If American militia have already fired on British soldiers, then England's liable to want to punish all the colonies," Andrew said.

"You'd sure think so! They can't let this happen in one colony, or they know that it'll happen everywhere else they try to take our weapons from us. This looks bad, Andrew," Nathan said, his eyes solemn.

"I guess it does. I've asked Father what war with England will do to his shipping business, but he just says that war will hurt everyone. He doesn't really answer."

The trap was sprung without warning. Four horsemen dashed out of the woods just thirty yards ahead of the two boys, and with pistols in hand yelled for them to halt.

Instinctively Andrew hauled his horse's head to the right, kicked his flanks, and galloped into the woods. "Run, Nathan!" he called.

"Those are Morgan's men!"

Nathan kicked and turned his horse and dashed into the forest behind Andrew.

Both boys had recognized two of the men's horses as those they'd seen tied at the hitch-rail of Morgan's Tavern. Ducking low to avoid the branches of the trees, Nathan followed Andrew's mount in a dangerous race through the woods. A vine whipped his hat from his head, and another almost tore the long rifle from his grasp. Bending his body low over the horse's neck, he guided the galloping animal through the thick brush, dodging around trees, weaving through the forest to escape the pursuing riders behind.

Yelling with rage and frustration, the four men who'd sprung the trap rushed toward the spot where the boys had entered the forest, and plunged after them. The leader, a big man in blackened buckskins, shouted again for the boys to halt. Raising his pistol above his head, he fired a shot to scare them, then thrust the weapon into the saddle holster and pulled out another. "Stop! You boys stop!" Behind him the other three men raced their horses in single file through the thick trees and bush.

Andrew, in the lead, ducked another branch but failed to see a small trench in the ground ahead. His mount plunged down suddenly, struggled to regain his footing, then scrambled up, almost throwing Andrew off. Desperately clinging to the animal's mane with his left hand, gripping his rifle in the other, Andrew hung on. Behind him, Nathan saw the trench in time to slow his mount and make a better crossing. Then they raced ahead through the treacherous woods in single file, spurred by the angry yells of the four horsemen.

Guiding the big mare around a thick cluster of trees, Andrew saw a path crossing from his right to his left. *That goes back to town!* he thought in a flash. Instantly he turned his horse to the left and galloped down the narrow trail, followed at once by Nathan on the gray. Thick leaf-covered branches clutched at their faces from either side as the boys raced through at a frantic pace.

Behind them, the leader of the pursuers failed to see the trench in time. His horse stumbled and went down, throwing its rider over his head and into the bank. The galloping men behind barely missed trampling the fallen horseman. One failed to avoid the now-riderless horse – his mount smashed into the frantic animal, and both went down in a tumble, tossing the rider onto the ground.

Shouting curses the leader had stumbled to his feet and sought his mount. The other fallen man staggered up also. But their horses were milling frantically in the woods, and would not come when called. Finally, the remaining two mounted men were able to gather them and lead them back to their shaken riders.

"Where'd those boys go?" the big man in black shouted, as he hauled himself into the saddle and wheeled his horse back in the direction the boys had taken.

But no one could answer him. The thick branches made difficult going for the pursuing men, and before they reached the trail the boys had taken, the leader pulled up in confusion. "We'll never find them now!" a rider behind him yelled.

"Then back to the road!" the leader shouted. "We'll get back there and catch them before they get to Williamsburg."

"We can't get them close to the town!" another called. "We'll be spotted, and you know what the patriot committee will do to us if we're caught! They'll tar and feather us and maybe put us in the stocks!"

"We can't fail!" the leader shouted. "Morgan wants us to question those boys about the messages they carried! We'll catch them before they get to town and make them talk!"

"And we'll rough 'em up for making us fall!" a man called, as the four raced back to the road in single file.

But Andrew and Nathan were galloping at full speed along the narrow path that seemed to parallel the road. "This goes to town!" Nathan called. "I know it now!"

"Then we'll beat those men back!" Andrew replied gratefully. "Gosh, that was close!"

"If they'd waited till we were ten yards closer, we might not have made it." Nathan said. "That was quick thinking, Andrew!"

"We're not back yet," Andrew said grimly, ducking another branch that almost knocked him from his horse. "Watch out!" he called back.

But Nathan had seen Andrew bend low over the horse's neck, so he was ready for the branch when he reached it. Doggedly the boys raced their mounts along the trail, praying that they'd reach the outskirts of town before their pursuers caught up with them.

"Can you see anyone behind you?" Andrew called back over his shoulder.

But Nathan had been glancing back repeatedly and had seen nothing.

"Nope – nothing, thank the Lord! I haven't heard them either."

Finally the trail opened into a wide field. Houses were visible on the far side, and several riders. "We made it!" Andrew sighed gratefully, slowing his mount and letting Nathan ride up beside him. "Where's your hat?" he asked, as he looked over and saw Nathan bareheaded.

"Knocked off by one of those branches," Nathan replied with a grin. "At least it didn't take off my head! Where'd you get that cut on your face?"

Andrew felt his check, drew his hand away, and saw blood. "Gosh, I don't know! I never felt it!"

"What did those men want?" Nathan asked, puzzled. "They're taking a chance trying to grab us like that!"

"I guess they want us to tell them what was in the messages we carried the other day," Andrew replied. "That really seemed to matter to them. I guess that's why Zed and that other man tried to capture me!"

"Things are getting bad, Andrew," Nathan said solemnly, his eyes sad now. "This kind of thing shouldn't happen. It's almost like the British have already declared war on us."

"Well, the Governor has, by stealing our powder." Andrew answered. "No one's safe now, I guess."

They passed houses now, and people, and began to feel secure for the moment. Then they rode past the College, turned onto Duke of Gloucester Street, and headed home.

Chapter Ten

"CAPTURE THOSE GIRLS!"

The next day, Sarah Edwards and Rachel Hendricks hurried along the busy Duke of Gloucester Street to the small wooden building that housed the Printing Office and Bookbindery, and which also served as the city's Post Office. They'd been sent by their fathers to mail some letters. When they arrived, the girls found the two doors of the building crowded with people, eagerly reading and discussing the latest news from the northern colonies. Just in front of Mr. Dixon's house next door, waited a carriage with an elegantly dressed driver holding the reins of two magnificent brown horses. Beside the carriage, talking with the driver, stood two large men wearing the uniform of the Governor's staff.

Because of the people crowding to enter the building, Sarah and Rachel had to wait for several minutes before they were able to mount the step and go in. Once inside, they waited again, as those in front of them looked over various papers and books, and posted letters to be mailed out of town.

Sarah and Rachel loved this store. Here's where they'd often bought books and stationery, and pored over other books they couldn't afford. Here they'd also heard much of the town

gossip. Today they would learn far more than they had expected!

As Sarah and Rachel waited to post their letters, two richly
dressed middle-aged ladies in the small room to the girls' left
were engaged in animated conversation. "I tell you, Mary,"
one of them was saying in a loud whisper which immediately
caught Sarah's attention, "the Governor will not put up with
this rebellious activity any longer! I know for a fact that he's
planning to arrest that traitor Patrick Henry for inciting rebellion against the King. And he's not going to let those men the
Virginians have elected go to Philadelphia for their Continental
Congress!"

Shocked, Sarah grabbed Rachel's arm, and drew her toward
the narrow door that led to the side room in which the two ladies
were standing. Surprised at Sarah's action, and still holding
the leather-bound cookbook she'd been reading, Rachel allowed Sarah to lead her closer to the doorway that separated
the two rooms. Inside the next room, the two ladies continued
their whispering, but with the carelessness of those who habitu-
ally cared not what their servants heard them say.

"Well, I am certainly glad to hear that," the second lady was
saying. She was a stout woman, with an elaborate hair-do in
the latest style, wearing a brilliant pink dress, and she shook
her head in anger at the thought of colonial resistance to British
policies. "My husband told me this morning that things are
very serious, and that if England doesn't take a firm position
now, the colonies could easily separate, and form their own
independent governments."

Sarah recognized the second speaker as Mrs. Granville,
whose husband was a close friend of Governor Dunmore. The

other lady, tall, and wearing a deep blue dress, was unknown to her. As the ladies continued talking, Sarah realized that she **had** to get all the information she could and pass this on to her father.

"Let's look at these books," she said quietly to Rachel, squeezing her way to the counter where new books were stacked. Now she was right at the open doorway to the small room, directly in sight of the two ladies. She picked up a slim book of poetry and opened its pages at random, careful to keep her head down and her eyes on the pages before her. Rachel was puzzled at her friend's actions; she'd been listening to the men ahead of her discuss a book on history, and hadn't heard the words that had so alarmed Sarah. But she followed Sarah to the narrow counter, large brown eyes wide with curiosity. From where she was standing, Rachel couldn't see the ladies Sarah had overheard.

"Why did you come over here?" she whispered.

"I want to hear what those ladies are saying," Sarah whispered back. Standing near the door, Sarah could keep the ladies in sight. But now they were close enough to the two women so that Rachel also could hear their words in spite of the various conversations occurring between the other customers in the Printing Office. Mrs. Granville repeated her statement that the Governor had threatened to arrest Patrick Henry. Then her companion stated emphatically that Governor Dunmore was sending messages to the various magistrates in Virginia to prevent the delegates from attending the Continental Congress in Philadelphia.

"All the colonies seem to be planning rebellion!" Mrs. Granville replied in outrage, shaking her head at the thought.

As if conscious that they were carelessly repeating confidential information in a very public place, the women suddenly stopped talking. Mrs. Granville looked sharply toward the open door, and was shocked at what she saw. Staring directly at her with wide blue eyes stood a young girl in a blue dress with long white apron and white cap. The girl's lips were parted in surprise at the words she'd just heard the ladies exchange.

Sarah's face flushed as the woman looked into her eyes. *She knows I heard her!* she thought frantically. Hurriedly Sarah dropped her eyes to the book in her hand, and tried to pretend to read. "Look, Rachel," she said, "here's a poem I like!"

Would the women overlook her interest? Her heart was pounding, and her breathing became rapid. What would those ladies do if they suspected that she'd learned of the Governor's plans? Her hand shook as she held the book for Rachel to read.

With her eyes on the opened pages before her Sarah couldn't see the shock on Mrs. Granville's face. The woman **knew** that Sarah had heard her conversation. Setting her mouth in a grim line, Mrs. Granville turned back to her friend and frowned a warning. Startled, the other woman looked toward Sarah who was standing just a few feet away. Now she too was shocked, knowing that the young girl could have heard all their words about the Governor's plans against Patrick Henry and the Virginia delegates to the Continental Congress in Philadelphia.

Mrs. Granville jerked her head towards the door, and hurried out, followed closely by her companion. Their carriage was waiting outside to their right, and the two ladies walked quickly toward it. The two men in the uniform of the Governor's servants saw them coming, and backed respectfully away. But

Rachel and Sarah overhear the plot to arrest Patrick Henry.

the two ladies went up to these servants and began to whisper anxiously, glancing back at the Post Office as they did so.

Very nervous now that the women had left so abruptly, Sarah whispered to Rachel in a shaking voice: "She knows that I heard her!" Her heart was beating rapidly, her face was flushed, and she wondered what she should do. The book of poetry was shaking in her hand.

"We've got to stay here and finish our business," Rachel said shrewdly, "so we won't seem suspicious. I'll mail the letters and you keep reading." Rachel returned to the counter and waited to be served. Behind Rachel now and to her left, at the narrow counter lined with books, Sarah stood perfectly still, pretending to read the book in her trembling hand.

Suddenly a man came up close beside her, picked up a book from the counter, and began to read. Sarah didn't dare move. She wondered if Mrs. Granville had sent the man to catch her. *Oh, Lord,* she prayed, *please help us get away!*

Then, through the open door of the Printing Office, Sarah heard a carriage drive off. Gradually, the thudding of her heart subsided. *Maybe those ladies hadn't gotten suspicious after all!* she thought to herself. *Now Rachel and I can hurry home and tell this news to our fathers!* As if to encourage Sarah that she was now safe, the man beside her moved on casually, taking no notice of her at all. She began to breathe more easily, and her heart rate slowed. But her face was still flushed, and anyone looking closely at her would be able to tell that she was terribly disturbed.

Finally the man behind the counter took the letters Rachel handed him. She paid what he asked, then turned breathlessly and moved through the crowded room back toward Sarah. She found her at the narrow counter, still pretending to concentrate on the book of poetry.

Rachel came and stood close beside her. "I finished," she said in a low voice. "Should we go now?"

"Maybe so," Sarah said, glancing around to see who might be listening. "But first, go see if those ladies are gone. I heard a carriage drive off, but I didn't dare turn and look." Her voice was shaking.

Rachel was also alarmed. Peering past her friend's shoulder, she looked through the window. But the view was too narrow for her to see the carriage. She stepped closer to the glass and glanced at the street. The carriage was gone! Turning, she moved back to stand beside Sarah.

"I don't see a carriage there now," she said. "They must have gone!"

"Thank the Lord for that!" Sarah exclaimed fervently. "We've got to get home at once! Let's go straight across the street. But we can't look around – we've got to pretend we're just having fun and aren't worried about anything!"

Stepping quickly out the door of the Printing Office, the two girls descended the narrow step and walked rapidly under a large tree toward the broad dirt road. But just as they were about to step into the street, a long freight wagon pulled to a stop just in front of them, blocking their way. Sarah turned to her left and led her friend around the horses that pulled the wagon. The two girls stepped into the broad dirt road and began to cross.

Suddenly a group of riders approached rapidly along the street from their right, their horses kicking up clouds of dust. The girls stopped, waited for these to pass, then walked quickly across to the south side of Duke of Gloucester Street. Stepping up to the rough walk in front of the stores on that side of the street, they turned left and hurried along in the direction of the Capitol Building. They talked animatedly as they moved, hoping that those ladies hadn't sent anyone to stop and question them.

But Mrs. Granville **had** done just that: she'd sent the Governor's two servants to stop the girls and find out just what they'd heard in the Printing Office! When Sarah and Rachel left the store so rapidly, however, then dodged around the long freight wagon, the servants lost sight of the girls for a moment. Puzzled, the men halted, searching for Sarah and Rachel amid the crowd of people. Then the three galloping riders distracted them for another moment, and by the time they'd spotted the two girls already across the street, the men realized that they'd have to hurry to catch up with them. Cursing, the Governor's men dashed toward the street in pursuit.

But they were stopped again! Two long wagons, each pulled by six horses, moved quickly in front of them, forcing the men to halt. Now the girls had gotten a clear lead. Enraged now, the Governor's servants waited for the wagons to pass, then ran to the other side of Duke of Gloucester Street in desperate pursuit of Sarah and Rachel. Running along the unpaved walkway, they slowed when a thick cluster of men blocked their path. But they could see the girls ahead of them on the walk, and they were not far away!

"We've got them!" the big man said to his companion as they threaded their way through a crowd of men. Sarah and

Rachel were now in sight of their two pursuers, and just about to pass a row of horses tethered to the hitching rail in front of James Anderson's house.

Chapter Eleven

"RUN!"

Very frightened now by the close pursuit of the Governor's two men, Sarah and Rachel hurried past the main door of James Anderson's house. Here a crowd of men, black and white, were gathered in small groups. Anderson's seven forges were always busy, turning out the metal work necessary for the town's economy, and the air was rent by the sounds of hammers pounding on iron as well as the shouting and laughter of the men. Nervous, stamping horses waited to be shoed, their tails swishing madly at the swarms of flies that tormented them. Standing in front of the store, groups of men were buying guns and tools and showing these to each other.

Frantic now, fearing that the Governor's servants might be able to catch up with them, Sarah and Rachel weaved their way through the clusters of men, barely avoiding a large pool of muddy water beside the walkway. As they did so, Rachel threw a frightened glance over her shoulder – their pursuers were almost upon them! Heart beating nervously, she followed Sarah past a huge brown stallion tied to the hitching rail alongside the walk. Suddenly on the ground before her she saw a large sheet of newspaper. Quickly Rachel stooped, picked up the newspaper, and waved it wildly in front of the tethered brown stallion.

Snorting with surprise, the large beast reared violently up and back to the length of its tether – right into the Governor's servants! The rear quarters of the big horse slammed into the two uniformed men and knocked them both into the long muddy pool they'd just skirted. Dirty water splashed out in all directions as the two men crashed flat on their backs, arms wide, yelling as they hit.

Startled crowds of men looked around, saw the two men struggling in the mud and water, and began to laugh. Now the girls rushed ahead, hurrying to get away while their pursuers were still on the ground.

Sarah and Rachel were so engrossed in getting through the crowd of men that they whisked right by Andrew and Nathan without even seeing them! The boys had just emerged from Geddy's store when the fleeing girls rushed past. Startled, Andrew called out in surprise, but Sarah and Rachel, not recognizing his voice in their fright, rushed on.

"Well, there sure are some conceited girls around town these days!" Andrew said with a serious look on his face, as he and Nathan dashed along the walkway and caught up with Sarah and Rachel. "They won't even speak to their friends or their neighbors!"

He looked reproachfully into Sarah's wide eyes.

"They won't even speak to their **brothers**!" Nathan added.

"Oh," Sarah said in confusion as she glanced up and recognized the boys, "we didn't see you!"

But she and Rachel continued to hurry along, and the boys had to move fast to keep up with them.

"Well, if we're that insignificant..." Andrew began.

But Sarah interrupted him. "We've heard some awful news! We've got to get home and tell Father!"

"And the Governor's men are chasing us!" Rachel added, her brown eyes wide with fright. "I scared that big horse into them, but they'll catch us if we don't run!"

Sobered by the girls' earnestness, Andrew and Nathan stopped their teasing, and began to walk quickly beside the girls.

"Let's get away from the street!" Sarah said. "We can't let anyone hear us!"

A number of men, many of them servants and slaves, were passing along the dusty path in front of the shops and houses that lined the street. Sarah knew that some one would overhear them if they didn't get away from the crowds.

"Sarah," Rachel said suddenly, "those men are after us again!" Sarah looked back and saw the two mud-splattered servants charging after them through the crowds of startled men.

"Keep moving!" Nathan said quietly, "we'll think of something."

"But how can we get away from them?" Sarah asked apprehensively, glancing back at her brother. "If they stop us, what'll happen?"

"We won't let them stop you!" Andrew said as they hurriedly crossed Botetourt Street and passed John Tarpley's store.

"I've got an idea!" Andrew said suddenly. "Nathan and I will pretend to fight, then we'll bump into those men. You girls run through the yard of the tavern and get on home!"

"But what will happen to you and Nathan?" Rachel asked in consternation.

"Nothing," Nathan assured her. "We'll pretend to fight, like Andrew said, just long enough to distract them – by then you'll be out of sight. Then we'll take a round-a-bout way home."

"Hey!" a rough voice called behind them. "You girls, stop at once!"

"Don't run!" Andrew said quietly to Sarah. "Just keep walking fast."

Andrew stopped abruptly and grabbed Nathan by the front of his shirt. Glancing to his left, he saw the two men in the Governor's red uniforms almost upon them. He gave Nathan a violent shove that sent his friend reeling back into a hitch rail. Yelling with anger, Nathan rushed back at Andrew, swerved to his left at the last moment, then right, and rammed his head into his friend's stomach, driving him violently into the two startled pursuers.

Shouting with pretended anger, Andrew flung his strong arms out wide, catching one of the men a blow in the stomach with his elbow even as he fell backwards into the other. The man collapsed to the ground, with Andrew falling on top of him, while the other doubled over, hands clasped to his stomach.

Nathan rushed again at Andrew, as if to strike him while he was down. Instead, he grabbed Andrew's wrist and pulled him off the Governor's prostrate servant. That man was groaning and clutching his ribs where Andrew's full weight had crashed into him.

The boys began yelling at each other, a crowd of men gathered, and the Governor's two men were effectively distracted from the pursuit of Sarah and Rachel. By the time the groaning man had struggled to his feet, his companion began to advance threateningly towards Andrew and Nathan.

The two boys whirled then and ran into the yard behind Anderson's buildings. The Governor's men started to follow, then realized that they'd lost sight of the girls. Cursing wildly, they looked down the street toward the Capitol where they'd last seen Sarah and Rachel rushing away.

But the girls were no longer in sight! While Andrew and Nathan were pretending to fight, Sarah and Rachel had ducked through the yard of the tavern and raced past the outbuildings in the yard, hurrying toward Francis Street.

Looking back toward the two boys who'd just spoiled their mission of stopping the girls, the Governor's mud-splattered frustrated men were just in time to see Andrew and Nathan disappear into the crowds of men in front of the store.

The boys ran into the yard behind the store, past surprised servants, dodging behind outbuildings and the garden, until they came to the picket fence at the back. Leaping easily over the fence the two turned left and ran along Francis Street. Some distance ahead of them they saw the two girls hurrying home.

"We've got to stay between the girls and those men in case they come through this far!" Andrew said as they slowed their pace along the dirt path beside the street, scattering a flock of squawking chickens.

"I don't think they know where to look," Nathan replied. "The girls were already out of their sight when I pulled you up! That was a great idea, Andrew!" he said admiringly.

"I'm sure glad I thought of it!" Andrew said. "We couldn't let those men grab Sarah and Rachel and question them!"

"But what could they have done?" Nathan asked. "They just can't capture people in the street like that!" He stumbled suddenly as his foot landed in a pothole, but recovered quickly.

"I don't know, but we don't want the girls caught in anything that makes the Governor mad at them – and at our families!"

"What do you think Sarah and Rachel did to cause those men to chase them?" Nathan asked, wondering.

"No telling!" his friend replied. Ahead of them, the two girls ducked between two houses. Looking back over his shoulder, Andrew saw no signs of the Governor's servants. "I don't see those men. I think the girls are clear. Let's cut through this path and get off this street while we're out of their sight!"

The boys turned right and ran through a path between a field and a fenced-in yard. Under tall trees they sprinted, until they came to the next dirt road. Here they slowed, and stopped.

"Gosh, that was a good run!" Andrew said, breathing deeply and breaking into a broad grin. "But did you have to ram me in the stomach with all your might like that? You could have killed me right there!"

"That wasn't all my might; it wasn't even half my strength!" Nathan said, grinning back. "Besides, we had to make it look **real**, didn't we?"

"Well, you made it look **real** enough," Andrew agreed. "It **felt** real too! And I **really** caught that man's stomach with my elbow when I fell on him!"

"You knocked the breath out of him!" Nathan agreed. "He got up mighty slow! Now we'd better get back home and learn what troubles those girls got into!"

The boys broke into a run again. What had Sarah and Rachel done to cause the Governor's men to pursue them?

Chapter Twelve

"GET THAT BOY!"

The large, athletic, red-faced man in the elegant attire of the Royal Governor sat in his chambers in the Capitol building, flanked on one side by a captain of marines, and on the other by a lieutenant of infantry. Across the table from them stood two terrified men, twisting hats uncomfortably in their hands under the tongue-lashing the Governor and his advisors had been giving them.

"How could three men let two half-grown boys get out of a tavern with those letters to the rebel leaders?" the Governor demanded again, pounding his fist on the thick wooden table. A powerfully built Scotsman, Lord Dunmore was a skilled horseman and hunter. As a man of action he was finding it incomprehensible that these two men quivering before his rage had allowed the boys to escape.

"Sir," Zed replied, his massive frame wilting under the murderous glare of the Royal Governor, "they surprised us. I was yanking one of those kids out of the booth when he hit me with the tankard. It caught me unexpected-like, and when he hit me again I just went down." His nose was covered by an unsightly dirty bandage, and a huge lump disfigured the right side of his head.

"But you and Morgan were right there, Silas!" The Governor said angrily, turning to the small man dressed in black. "Why in heaven's name didn't you do something?"

"Like Zed said, sir," Silas replied, licking his lips nervously as the most powerful man in the Colony of Virginia bored angry eyes into him, "that boy drew a tomahawk quicker than lightning. He was ready to throw! He was scared, and he would have killed the first one of us that moved. Then while we were figurin' what to do about him, the other boy cocked his rifle and aimed it at us – we hadn't even seen him grab it! – everything happened so sudden-like, and..."

"Enough! Enough!" the Governor said tiredly, turning to the officer of marines. "Captain, we've **got** to get one of those letters! We've **got** to know what the rebels are planning! And we've **got** to get a list of all the men who are getting those letters!"

"Sir," Silas interjected nervously, licking his lips again, twisting his wide-brimmed black hat in his hands, "I think we can do that for you."

"How?" the Governor barked.

"Morgan knew one of those boys, sir," Silas replied. "He remembered his name after they rode away. We can get one of those boys and bring him here."

"That's the stupidest thing you've said yet!" the captain of marines said threateningly, leaning forward, a long white scar on his face highlighting the angry red of his countenance. "What would these Virginians do if they thought the Governor was kidnapping their children? Don't you know that the Americans are armed?" He turned in disgust and addressed the Governor. "Your Excellency, these two men are so stupid they're dangerous! We'd better get rid of them and find other men to do what must be done!"

"No! Please, sir!" Silas said, his pale face even whiter with fear now. "Give us another chance! We can do this for you! We can get one of those kids and question him ourselves. Then we'll know the names of the men they took those letters to. We won't bring him here!"

Lord Dunmore said nothing. For a long moment he just stared at the two men standing before him. A clock in the corner ticked loudly as the Governor made up his mind.

Zed said nothing. His skill was in his brute strength, not his mind. He knew this, and knew he'd better keep his mouth shut.

Groaning heavily, the Governor made up his mind. "All right," he said. "One more chance. You get one of those boys and make him talk. Make him tell you what those letters said – he has to know that. Make him tell you the names of the men to whom they were delivered. Then let him go! Then get back here at once." He stared grimly at Silas and Zed in turn.

"Yes, sir!" Silas replied fervently. "We'll get one of those boys, Governor! And we'll make him talk! I promise!"

"Get out," Lord Dunmore said with a weary wave of his hand. Silas and Zed hurried out of the room.

The two men hastened to their horses, mounted, and rode off at a gallop.

"Where we goin'?" Zed asked as they swerved around the cannons in front of the Governor's Palace and thundered down the Palace Green towards Duke of Gloucester Street.

"To the cabin," the grim-faced Silas replied. "We've got to plan this with care. We know where the Hendricks boy lives – he's the one that hit you! We'll plan what to do, then scout his house after dark."

"Why don't we go grab him now?" Zed asked. He'd like nothing better than to beat up that boy who'd knocked him out and broken his nose.

"Because we'd be shot, that's why!" Silas retorted in astonishment. "Why don't you think a minute! We can't grab him in broad daylight! We've got to scout his place at dark, then take him when he's by himself."

After dark the two men rode back into town, crossed the Duke of Gloucester Street, skirted the tall brick Powder Magazine, then turned and headed toward William Hendricks' house.

"Lots of men out tonight!" Zed said quietly to Silas as the two set their horses in a leisurely walk along the rough road. They knew they had to move slowly so as not to attract any attention to themselves.

"Yeah!" Silas agreed nervously. *Too many men!* he thought. But the darkness prevented anyone from seeing their faces, and they'd changed horses as well. No one should recognize them, he hoped. "We'll tie the horses in that clump of trees not far from Hendricks' house, then wait for our chance to grab the boy."

"Should be easy," Zed said grimly. He had plans for Andrew; he meant to make him pay for breaking his nose.

They passed several houses, then came to a wide field dotted with trees. Dismounting, they tied their horses to a tree and began to walk toward their target. Passing several houses they approached Hendricks' house – and stopped in surprise. Tied to the rail before that house and the one before it were more than a dozen horses!

"What's going on?" Zed asked in surprise.

"I don't know, but there's a crowd of men there," Silas replied anxiously. "We've got to be careful!"

Just then they heard the sound of approaching hoof beats. A man rode past them, swung from the saddle, tied his horse to the rail, and hurried up to Hendricks' door. Silas and Zed were now between Nelson Edwards' home and the Hendricks'. They saw the door open for the late arrival, and before it closed they both recognized the one who'd let the man in the house.

"There's that boy!" Zed hissed in rage, halting in his tracks. "That's him!"

"I saw him!" Silas agreed, grabbing the big man's arm and urging him forward. "But keep walking; we don't want to look suspicious!" The two resumed their pace and walked by the Hendricks' home. No one seemed to have noticed them.

"What are we going to do now?" Zed asked, stumbling over a tree root and recovering quickly. His massive frame towered above that of his companion and he was longing to show his rage in violent action against the boy who'd knocked him down and broken his nose.

"We've got to sneak up to a window and listen to what's going on!" Silas replied instantly. "That's the only way we can get close to that boy."

"Maybe they've got a dog," Zed said.

"Not outside, they don't," Silas said confidently. "Not with all those men coming. They've put their dog up."

The two walked past the corner of the picket fence, ducked behind a tall oak, and looked anxiously around. "I don't see anyone else coming," Silas said, "but that doesn't mean they won't. We'll sneak up to the west side of the house and hide in those bushes under the window. Maybe we can hear what they're saying from there."

They climbed the fence with difficulty, then crept cautiously through the darkness toward the house. Lights poured from the windows and made slanting patches on the dark ground. Carefully avoiding these patches of light, the two slid through the shadows. When they got close to the house, they could hear men talking.

Inside, William Hendricks looked at the two dozen men packed into his long dining room. Half of them were seated, the rest were standing against the walls. Most held a mug of hot chocolate or coffee which Carolyn Hendricks, Mary Edwards and their daughters had been filling for them. Candles burned in their rounded glass frames hung on the wall, throwing light on the group. Some of the men were smoking, making the room stuffy, so William Hendricks had opened the windows to let in fresh air.

To the great delight of the boys, their fathers had allowed Andrew and Nathan to join the men. They were standing, jammed against the wall beside their fathers, listening to the men talk. They were all waiting for their visitor to tell his tale.

The assembled men had just heard Sarah and Rachel tell what they'd overheard from the ladies in the Post Office. They'd been astounded to learn that the Governor was planning to stop the Virginia delegates from attending the Continental Congress in Philadelphia. They were even more shocked when Sarah had told them he also wanted to arrest Patrick Henry.

When Sarah and Rachel had finished their story, and joined their mothers in the kitchen, one of the men spoke to Hendricks and Edwards. "What girls you've raised! They were brave – and smart – to get that information, and bring it back to us!"

"And smart to escape like they did!" another added. "Scaring that horse was a brilliant idea!"

"If a twelve year old girl can ferret out the Governor's plans," another said, "and her eleven year old friend can knock down the Governor's two henchmen, then surely our militia can stand up to Governor Dunmore!" The men laughed in hearty agreement.

"Well, gentlemen," Hendricks said, standing against the wall next to the kitchen door, "it makes us realize that the troubles we're about to hear of in Massachusetts may soon be ours." He turned to a man seated to his left. "This is Ebenezer Cuthburt, from Lexington, in Massachusetts. He's a business colleague of mine and Nelson's, just come from Philadelphia on our schooner, and he's anxious to tell Virginians about the fight his militia had with the British army."

The room grew completely silent as the Virginians gave the man from Massachusetts their complete attention. Ebenezer Cuthburt rose and faced them. Stocky, powerfully built, dressed in dark coat and trousers, he had thick black hair above his wide red face – a solemn-seeming man, Andrew had thought as he'd met him that evening. Gray eyes shone under bushy black eyebrows as he addressed the now-silent Virginians.

"Thanks, William. And thank you, gentlemen, for coming. We can't tell you how grateful we are for the prayers, the letters and the supplies you people in the southern colonies have given us, especially Boston, this past year. When the British Navy closed our port, thousands of people were thrown out of work. The food you southerners have sent us has helped many a family, and we thank God constantly for your generosity." He paused then, shifted his balance with some difficulty, and winced with pain.

"Ebenezer, sit down!" William Hendricks said quickly. "We can all hear you just as well from a chair."

"Thanks, William, but I'll stand. It was just a grazing shot, thankfully."

The Virginians were silent. Here was a man who'd already fought the British, and been wounded in the struggle for liberty. Their faces were grave as he continued.

"You know that the British are shipping fourteen regiments of their regular army to Boston." He paused, then explained the significance of that. "That's maybe eight or nine thousand men – and we know they mean to conquer us. So thousands of us, in all the northern colonies, have been drilling and training for what we know is coming. Like you people in Virginia, every one of our counties has formed a militia company."

He smiled for the first time. "We've got a lot of help. That is, we've got people who know how to get information about the British plans. They tell us what the British leaders are going to do before they do it. And they told us that the English General Gage planned to send some hundreds of soldiers to capture the powder and other equipment we'd stored for our militia in Concord."

He stopped a moment, and the Virginians couldn't help but think of the action of their own Governor Dunmore; he'd also sent troops to steal the Virginian's powder. And he got away with it: the marines had stolen part of the powder stored in the Magazine before the night watchman had alerted the town. The Virginians' faces were grim as they listened to Cuthburt resume his story.

"They also had orders to capture some of our leaders so they could ship them back to England for trial!"

The men murmured among themselves at that; they knew what that meant. In case they didn't, Cuthburt explained the matter. "That means they'd be tried in England, by an English jury. None of their own peers would be there. None of their own witnesses could get there to testify in their defense. None of their fellow-citizens would be present to help them get a fair trial – only a jury of hostile Englanders who'd do just what the English government told them to."

"We all know what the government would tell them to do," one of the men standing said quietly. "They'd tell them to find them guilty of treason and hang them!"

"That would be no trial, then," said another. "It'd just be murder!"

Cuthburt nodded his head solemnly. "That's right! It would! The British Secretary of State, the Earl of Darmouth, ordered Gage to strike quickly, before we were trained and properly equipped to face the English soldiers. So Gage ordered the Grenadiers and the Light Infantry, about seven hundred men altogether, to do the job: to destroy our munitions and equipment at Concord, and seize some of our leaders. On the 18th of April, the soldiers marched to the waterfront and were rowed across the Charles River. They got wet, too," he chuckled, "because they had to wade up to their knees and then stand for hours in their wet boots until their provisions were landed!"

"Were your militia warned they were coming?" Nelson Edwards asked quietly, as the assembled men smiled at the discomfort suffered by the British troops.

"They sure were!" Cuthburt replied with a grim smile. "We've got people who find out these things for us! When the British closed the port of Boston, they threw a lot of men out of work. Those men are eager to help us now. Also, some of our leaders set up a system to watch for the British to make any offensive moves. Dr. Joseph Warren and Mr. Paul Revere knew something was brewing when they saw the English transports moving in the harbor on April 15, so they rode to Lexington and Concord and warned our militia."

He shook his head in wonder. "Funny thing, though. It didn't seem to occur to the British General Gage that we might be watching the movements of his forces! Most professional British army officers don't credit Americans with any brains at all! But when he sent out mounted scouts to seal the roads, we knew something was about to happen. Then he moved one of his warships in the harbor nearer to the shore. So Paul Revere was rowed across the Charles River even while the British soldiers were being ferried across too. Another of our men got out of town by a different route. Both hurried into the counties with the news of the British march."

He staggered then, and winced. Instantly Hendricks pushed a chair behind his legs, and forced him to sit down. Gratefully, Cuthburt sat, with an apologetic look on his face. "Guess I'm not as recovered as I thought I was," he said.

Grim-faced, the men waited silently for him to continue.

Chapter Thirteen

THE BATTLE OF LEXINGTON

Outside, Silas cursed silently. He couldn't understand all of the men's words inside the house. "We've got to get closer," he hissed to Zed, "'cause I can't catch all that they're saying."

"Those bushes aren't big enough to cover me," Zed protested in a whisper.

"Then stay here while I crawl under them. But I've got to hear what that man is saying. He's a Yankee – I can tell from his accent. And he's telling those men something important. We've got to learn what it is so's we can tell the Governor."

Carefully Silas snaked closer to the house. Inching under a clump of bushes next to the wall, he doubled up his legs so they couldn't be seen in the light that fell from the window. Now he could hear the speaker clearly.

"John Parker's captain of our Lexington militia," Cuthburt was telling them. "Paul Revere rode into town around midnight, and told Adams and Hancock about the British raid. When Parker heard, he called us to the village green. We waited in the dark for an hour, but nothing happened, so he sent us home and told us to run back to the green if we heard the drums."

Andrew and Nathan were mesmerized as the tale continued. They could picture the marching British column of Grenadiers and Light Infantry, muskets sloped across their shoulders, packs on their backs, marching rapidly behind their mounted officers through the early morning darkness toward the colonists' arms depot just outside of Concord.

"We learned later that the British Colonel Smith had ordered his men not to fire on us, unless we fired on them," Cuthburt continued. "Then he sent Major Pitcairn, a marine, with six companies to capture the bridges beyond Concord. That's when Paul Revere was captured."

The men stirred. "What happened to him?" one of the men asked.

"They threatened him, but he wouldn't tell 'em what he was doing. He asked why they were out like this at night, and they said they were just looking for deserters from their army. He knew they were lying, and told them five hundred militia would march to meet them if they didn't go back. That's when they put a pistol to his head. But they let him go when they heard us fire our muskets when we disbanded, so he got away."

He paused again, and lit his pipe. "That news about five hundred militia scared Major Pitcairn, so he had his men load their muskets. But he told them not to shoot unless we shot first. By now, church bells were ringing in all the villages around, and signal guns were calling the militia companies to muster. The whole countryside was coming to life as the militia got word of the British troops. Then Pitcairn led his soldiers into Lexington."

The listening Virginians pictured in their minds the ensuing action. Seventy men formed in two ranks on the village green of Lexington, Massachusetts, Cuthburt told them. "We weren't going to shoot," he said. "We didn't really know what to do. We just knew we had to be there, and show them we were ready. Then, hundreds of Redcoats came marching into town, straight toward where we were standing. When they saw us, they lost control of themselves! They just went wild! Major Pitcairn and a couple of officers rode up and yelled at us to throw down our guns and leave. You see, they meant to disarm us!"

That shocked the Virginians – the British meant to disarm the citizens! They all knew what happened to a people who had no weapons to defend themselves. They leaned forward as Cuthburt's voice dropped. The man from Massachusetts continued his story, almost as if he'd forgotten they were there, as if he were just thinking out loud about what he'd seen only a couple of weeks before.

"Our captain told us not to fire, but to get out of there. So we turned and started to walk away. But this enraged the British major! He meant to take away our guns! So he told his men to take them from us! We were already walking away, and that's when the English fired on us. We were totally surprised! They fired a volley, yelled, fired again and again, and charged with their bayonets!"

The startled Americans scattered, Cuthburt told them, leaving eight men dead and ten wounded on the green. Major Pitcairn was now yelling to his soldiers to cease firing, but they wouldn't stop. A few of the Americans knelt, aimed, and fired back. They were hopelessly outnumbered, however, and gunned down or scattered.

"The British officers said later that they'd seen the flash of powder from a musket, and that's why their men were ordered to fire. But we think they're lying. They were just angered that we were there, that we had guns to defend ourselves, and that we wouldn't give up our guns. So when the officers got them under control, they gave three cheers, and marched off to Concord to destroy our cannons and stores. They knew they'd shamed us, and killed and wounded our men, and driven us from the field."

He paused, his face sad. He seemed to be seeing it as if he were still there. "Eighteen of our men were lying in the green. Eight of them were dead," he repeated.

Cuthburt stopped and relit his pipe with shaking hands. For a moment he was unable to speak. None of the Virginians said anything. Then he continued. "Funny thing; Major Pitcairn is a fine, good natured man. And he likes Americans. But he couldn't stand to see us with our guns. He didn't order the firing – no one knows who did! – and he tried to stop it sooner! But he went on with his job, on to Concord, to get our cannons and gunpowder."

Cuthburt paused again; then he looked slowly around the room at the faces of the Virginians. "And that's when we all knew we had to fight against our government, against England; because our government was fighting against us, its citizens, right in our own town. They meant to take away our guns, by killing us if necessary. And without our guns, we knew we'd just be slaves."

The group of solemn-faced men pondered this message. They all knew it was true. Once people in power could disarm their citizens, tyranny was unstoppable. No man would be able to protect his wife and children from evil people in the community – or in the government. Centuries of human history had proved over and over again that unarmed citizens are always helpless before violent men.

Then Cuthburt's face hardened. His voice did too. "So they scattered us and beat us at Lexington. But that was just the beginning."

The Virginians could feel the implacable resolve of the Massachusetts men as Cuthburt continued. "Because all the towns sent help. The British soldiers marched on to Concord and destroyed some of our cannons and stores. But when they started to march back to Boston, the whole country rose against them! Company after company of militia marched to attack them! We fought from houses, from fields, from bridges; we shot at them from the front, and we shot at them from the flanks. We shot at their rear-guard. In a few hours they were in a desperate plight!"

Putting their wounded in wagons, the now-exhausted British column marched doggedly along the narrow road, shot at from every side, struggling like a tortured red-colored snake as it worked its way through the countryside. "If General Gage hadn't sent a thousand men to their rescue, they'd have had to surrender, because they were almost out of ammunition! We fought them all the way back to Boston. We beat 'em, too! But our men couldn't face their two cannons; whenever they fired those, our men scattered. That's what saved them that day; it was their cannons."

"So American militia beat the British army," one man said quietly.

"American militia beat the British army," Cuthburt agreed. "The British couldn't believe it. They despise us, and swore we'd never stand up to their fire. They know different, now!"

"How many men did you lose altogether, Ebenezer?" Nelson Edwards asked.

"Ninety," the Yankee replied, his face sad. "We lost ninety men, maybe a couple more."

"How many did the British lose?" someone asked.

"Two hundred and seventy. They had almost seventeen hundred men in action. We killed seventy-some, wounded one hundred and seventy, and they said that twenty-six of their soldiers were missing. Actually, those men deserted to our side, but the British won't admit it. Lots of their soldiers want to desert, but they know they'll be killed as examples if they're caught trying."

Now all the men wanted to know what the Massachusetts patriots had decided to do after the battle.

"Well, our Provincial Congress met last week and called for fourteen-thousand six hundred troops to be raised. We think twice that many will be needed to beat the British in Boston. But the other colonies are raising troops too. We're blocking General Gage and his men in Boston so they can't go out to raid our towns. They can't get food from the countryside, either. Our militia companies surround the city on the land-ward side. We've got some cannons mounted on the hills around the town, and we're collecting more."

He took his pipe out of his mouth, paused a moment as he looked slowly around the room, then concluded. "It's war, gentlemen. England's declared war against us already – the King has. Question is, will we fight for our homes, or just become his slaves? That's the question you face too!"

"It certainly is!" William Hendricks agreed quietly, his face sad.

"But the British **got** our powder!" one of the men said bitterly.

"Well, they got a lot from the Magazine," Hendricks agreed. "Fortunately, our militia companies have a lot stored. But the British will get that too, if we let them. If we don't do anything about Dunmore's raid on the Magazine, they'll think they've got nothing to fear from us. They'll think they can do anything they want!"

A murmur of agreement greeted this announcement.

"But some of our leaders want us to trust the Governor!" a tall man leaning against the wall said quietly. "They want us to let them get away with this."

"Patrick Henry says we can't let them do it!" a lean man at the table said emphatically.

All eyes turned toward the speaker, a militia leader from Hanover County. "We had over a thousand men gathered in Fredericksburg this weekend, fourteen companies of militia, and Henry told us we should march on Williamsburg at once to make the Governor give us back the gunpowder he stole from the Magazine!"

"Henry's right, Seth!" Hendricks agreed. "How can we help him do it?" He turned to the others; "Seth's from the Hanover County militia. They're ready to fight now."

"Let me go back there and tell them Mr. Cuthburt's story," Seth replied. "The men from the western counties are ready to march. They need to hear about Lexington right away. Maybe that'll stiffen the spines of some of our men in Williamsburg and the Tidewater."

There was a stir at this remark. Everyone was aware that those living in the coastal regions had more to fear from immediate British reprisals, and were often more cautious than those in the western counties. Also, some of the more aristocratic families had such close family ties with the British Empire that they found it very difficult to think of actual war and separation.

Outside, crouched under the bushes, Silas smiled. He'd heard enough – and more than enough! Now he'd get back into favor with the Governor! This news would enable Dunmore to send soldiers to nab the patriots' messengers before they left Williamsburg! That'd stop their plans to resist before they were set in motion!

He began to crawl out from under the bushes; he had to rejoin Zed, and get this message to the Governor at once!

Inside, Hendricks turned to his son. "Andrew, ask your mother if those pies are ready."

"Yes, sir," Andrew replied. Entering the kitchen he relayed his father's question.

"They sure are, Andrew!" his mother replied with a smile. "They're outside on the back porch, cooling. You young folks can bring them in for us."

Rachel was taking pies out of their pots, but Laura, who'd just poured herself a mug of hot chocolate, turned toward the back door. Sarah had already jumped up and begun to follow Andrew.

Andrew grinned at Sarah as he brushed past, opened the back door, and stepped onto the porch – into the iron grip of Zed. The massive angry man had been standing beside the door with his back against the wall of the house, waiting for his chance to get Andrew. When Andrew stepped through the door, Zed grabbed him from behind, clapped a huge hand over his mouth, threw his strong arm around his chest, and began to carry the struggling boy off the porch.

Chapter Fourteen

"WE'VE GOT TO TELL PATRICK HENRY!"

Emerging onto the porch right behind Andrew, Sarah screamed at the sight of Andrew being carried off by a huge man. Instantly she ran and threw herself on the big man's back, clawing his face and eyes with all her strength.

Zed howled with pain and rage, dropping Andrew at once. Twisting his body frantically, he flung a massive arm around and threw Sarah off of him, off the porch, and onto the ground.

Laura, hearing Sarah's scream, rushed through the door in time to see the big man throw the younger girl off the porch. Instantly Laura flung her mug of steaming chocolate into Zed's face, and then threw the mug at his head. Zed screamed with pain and stumbled back, clawing at his face. Looking wildly around for a weapon, Laura saw the three-legged stool beside the door. She scooped this up and swung it with all her might against Zed's head.

Andrew, meanwhile, had stumbled off the porch and fallen to the ground when Sarah had attacked the big man. Heart pounding, adrenalin pumping, he turned in time to see Zed throw Sarah off the porch and onto the ground. Then he saw Laura strike Zed with the stool. The huge man reeled from the force of Laura's blow and staggered down the stairs. Rushing toward him, Andrew twisted on the ball of one foot as the Indians had taught him to do, and thrust his other heel with all the strength of his leg into the lower body of the battered man.

With a terrible gasp, Zed crumpled. But before he hit the ground, Andrew shifted his stance and slammed his right fist into Zed's jaw. When Zed fell flat, Andrew leaped, landing on his knees in Zed's back. The air whooshed from the stricken brute.

And now the yard was filled with men who'd poured out the back door when they'd heard Sarah's scream! Silas ran around the corner of the house – just in time to face William Hendricks' pistol! Rachel and Laura helped the stunned Sarah to her feet, and two men finally pulled Andrew away from pounding the inert body of the fallen Zed with his fists.

"What happened?" Rachel cried, as she and Laura led a shaken Sarah to the porch.

"I don't know!" Sarah sobbed, tears in her eyes, blood on her cheek where she'd struck the ground. "I just saw that big man grab Andrew! Where's Andrew?" she cried frantically.

"Here he is!" Nelson Edwards replied grimly, pulling the enraged boy to his feet and turning him back toward the house. "He was trying to kill the man that hit you, Sarah!"

"Are you all right?" she cried, one hand held to her bleeding cheek.

"Yes!" he said, his body still shaking from pounding Zed. "Are you?"

Unable to say more, she nodded, still trembling from shock. Laura led her back into the kitchen.

Andrew turned back then, and looked at the prisoner – whom he recognized at once as the man he'd seen with Zed and Morgan in the tavern. The other men from the house quickly joined them, ringing Silas and the fallen Zed in a circle from which there was no escape.

Silas was trying to explain what he was doing running around Hendricks' house at night. When someone asked about Zed, he cried out, "I tell you, I don't know this man! I just heard a girl scream, and I ran to help!"

"He's lying!" Andrew called out. "He and that big man on the ground are spies for the Governor! We met them in Morgan's Tavern. They tried to take away the letters we were taking to the patriot leaders! They'd have got 'em, too, if Nathan hadn't put his rifle on those men!"

"Andrew's right!" Nathan said hotly, shocked at the violence that had felled his sister and his friend. "They're the Governor's men, all right! We thought they might shoot us as we escaped, so we threw away that big man's pistol!"

Stunned, Silas looked at Andrew, and at Nathan who'd just come to stand beside his friend. His jaw dropped, and he stood speechless, not knowing how to get out of this.

It didn't take any time for the patriots to decide what to do with Silas and Zed. "We'll take them to the committee," Nelson Edwards said. "They'll keep 'em until this business with the Governor is settled. Then we can prefer charges against them both, William, for attacking our children!"

"With pleasure," William Hendricks said grimly, pistol still aimed steadily at Silas's heart.

Inside the house, Sarah's mother was washing the blood off her daughter's face. "It's just a cut, Sarah," she said thankfully. "It'll heal shortly."

"Oh, Mama, I didn't have time to think! I saw that huge man carrying Andrew away. I think I hurt his eyes – I hope I did! It's the only way I could think of to make him let Andrew go!"

"That was the right thing to do, Sarah!" her mother agreed emphatically. "We women are not strong like men; we've got to do what we can, and what you did made him free Andrew. I'm so proud of you!" She wiped Sarah's eyes and face gently, and then hugged her.

Outside, Nathan asked Andrew what had happened.

"I just stepped outside on the porch, and he grabbed me from behind. I didn't know what was happening! Then Sarah screamed, and threw herself on him and that made him yell and toss me down! She hurt him! When I was getting up from the ground I saw Laura hit him a terrific whack with a stool. That's all that saved me!" Andrew shuddered at the thought of almost being kidnapped by Zed.

"How'd you put him on the ground?" Nathan asked, awed.

"Well, when Laura smacked him on the head with that stool, he stumbled down the steps toward me, grabbing his face. So I ran at him and kicked him low, just like Moses and Abraham taught us," Andrew replied. "I kicked him as hard as I could, then hit him on the jaw when he fell. Then I jumped on his back." Andrew's chest was still heaving with his labored breathing.

"Gosh, Nathan," Andrew continued, "I wanted to kill him for hurting Sarah!" Never had Andrew known such anger, and it scared him.

"You didn't kill him," his father said suddenly as he came up beside his son and put his arm around his shoulders. "But between you and Sarah and Laura, he's in pretty bad shape! His face and head are bleeding, his jaw looks broken, and you hurt his back. He's still unconscious. And he deserved it all!"

Andrew's father regarded the big form lying motionless on the ground. "So that's the man that tried to hurt you in Morgan's Tavern, is it?"

"Yes, sir," Nathan replied. "That's him! We knew he'd have it in for Andrew."

William Hendricks reminded them of the meeting. "Let's go back inside and plan what to do about Ebenezer's report!"

"Maybe we'd better set someone to guard the house while we're meeting," Seth suggested.

"I'll do that," a stout man volunteered. "I grabbed my rifle when we ran out here. I'll patrol while you plan."

"Thanks, Walter," Hendricks said.

The men returned to the house, trooped through the kitchen, and into the dining room. Here they found plates with thick slices of pie for all of them. Half of the men sat at the table, the others stood, and all devoured the fresh pies that the ladies and girls had made.

"Mary's taken Sarah in her bedroom to wash the blood off her face," Carolyn Hendricks told her husband. "She's not really hurt – just stunned, and scared for Andrew."

"And well might she be!" he replied, shaking his head. "Imagine that this could happen in our own home!"

"That's what we said to ourselves in Lexington two weeks ago!" Ebenezer Cuthburt said solemnly. "How could soldiers be shooting at us, killing our people and stealing our property – right in front of our families, in our own town? But they did all that!"

"They'll do that and a lot more if we don't stop them!" Nelson Edwards said. Outraged at what Zed had done to Andrew and Sarah, he'd stayed to see that Silas and his accomplice were tied securely and put under guard, and he'd been the last to re-enter the house.

"But powerful men in Williamsburg and in the Tidewater don't want us to anger the Governor by demanding our powder back!" another man said, putting his empty plate on the table.

"We can't wait for them any longer!" William Hendricks insisted. "We've got to contact Patrick Henry. He's willing to do something!"

"He sure is!" Seth agreed. "That's what he told us this past weekend. 'We've got to do something,' he said, 'because Governor Dunmore will never return the gunpowder to us. We've got to take it back.' "

"Then let's make our plans," Hendricks said.

The meeting disbanded an hour later. The men dispersed, and began to ride back to their homes. Zed's unconscious body had been lifted with great difficulty onto a horse and carted off with Silas who, like his big companion, was tied hand and foot.

"We'll get them to the committee," Seth told Hendricks as they left. "They won't bother your boy again!"

"They'd better hope that these boys and girls don't bother **them**!" one of the men said, and the others laughed.

"I'd prefer charges against him tonight," Hendricks said grimly, "but these are the Governor's men. Dunmore would release them right away, and then he'd know all our plans. We can't let that happen!"

"Don't worry," Seth assured him. "Those two won't be freed until this business with the gunpowder is settled!"

Then they were gone. Nelson Edwards, William Hendricks and their sons turned back from the front door through which the men had just left, and went again to the dining room. Here, the two mothers were sitting with Laura, Sarah, and Rachel. Sarah was holding a bandage to the left side of her face, but seemed otherwise unhurt.

She smiled at Andrew as he came into the room, and he smiled back. He couldn't think of the right words – not with all those people in the room – so he just said, "Thanks!" to the brave girl. He knew that if she hadn't leaped on Zed, the big man would have taken him off the porch. Her attack had given Laura time to join in.

Then he looked at his older sister with awe. "Laura, that was a terrific hit you gave him with that stool!"

Laura was still outraged at what had happened. She'd cried when Andrew had come back on the porch, and her eyes were red. "I wanted to knock his head off his body!" she said fervently.

"You almost did!" her father smiled, putting his arms around her and pulling her head to his chest. "Laura and Sarah, you two are marvelous!"

"Time for us all to go to bed!" Nelson Edwards said decisively. "This has been a full evening!"

"Who's keeping Mr. Cuthburt?" Carolyn Hendricks asked.

"Mr. Wythe," her husband replied, still holding Laura.

"George Wythe is a great man," Nelson Edwards said quietly. "He's never wavered in all our struggles with the British Parliament."

"He is a great man," Hendricks agreed. "He's a man of principle and integrity. He knows that any government that exceeds it's constitutional limits is wrong, and he's always encouraged us to defend out families and our property against tyranny."

Mrs. Edwards rose to leave, and Sarah rose with her. Mrs. Hendricks followed them to the door. "How can I ever thank you for rescuing Andrew, Sarah?" she asked, giving the girl a grateful hug.

Sarah blushed, and told them goodnight as she followed her mother out the door. She glanced back as she left, smiled shyly at Andrew – then was gone.

"We'll talk tomorrow, William," Nelson Edwards said as he left. "We've done the right thing for now. Sending this message to Patrick Henry is the best thing that could have come from this meeting. He won't let us cave in to the Governor!"

"He's the man to lead us!" Hendricks agreed, shaking his friend's hand. "Good night."

Nelson and Nathan left for home, and William Hendricks closed the door behind them. He turned to his family and regarded them solemnly.

"Well, we can thank the Lord for protecting Andrew to-night."

"Amen!" his wife said fervently, hugging her son's shoulder.

"And we can thank Him for brave men in Massachusetts, who are willing to defend their homes and their families."

"And for brave men in Virginia, Father," Andrew said. "These men who were here tonight are willing to resist British tyranny too."

"They are indeed, Andrew," his father replied. "Let's gather around the table, and we'll read the Bible before we all go to bed."

Chapter Fifteen

PATRICK HENRY AND THE HANOVER MILITIA

Two days later, Andrew, Nathan, and Matthew Anderson galloped into the town of Newcastle, Virginia, with the dispatches from the Williamsburg patriots. Pulling up in front of the Court House in a swirl of dust, Anderson yelled to a group of armed men, "Where's Patrick Henry?"

"Inside the tavern!" a lean rifleman replied, pointing directly across the road. "They're having a council of war."

Without a word the three turned their horses toward the tavern, crossed the road, leaped from the saddles, tied their mounts to the rail and hurried inside. Groups of militia were drilling on the green and on the edges of the town. The sounds of other companies firing rifles and muskets came to their ears. The air was stirred by the beating of military drums.

On the long ride up from Williamsburg, the two boys had learned a great deal about Patrick Henry. "Known him for years," Anderson had told them. "We're going to Newcastle, and that's where Henry first set up in business. His father put him and his brother in a store, but they couldn't make a go of it."

Anderson had shaken his head at that. "Henry never belonged in a store! Not that he isn't a smart businessman; he is. But he's a great lawyer. He's honorable. He's down-to-earth. He cares for common people, for poor people, and he'll fight for anybody if he believes that their cause is right!"

Andrew and Nathan had plied the woodsman with questions about Henry as the three hurried their horses along the rough roads. The Williamsburg men believed that Patrick Henry was now their only hope if they wished to recover the colony's gunpowder and stand up to British tyranny. Matthew Anderson and the two boys were taking this message to Henry.

"Patrick Henry's about thirty-nine, I think," Anderson replied. "His store failed, like I said, and he tried another one. But he wasn't cut out for that. So he studied some books on law, rode to Williamsburg, got himself examined and licensed, and began to practice. And that's what he's done ever since."

"Father says he's the single most important man in the colonies' resistance to English tyranny," Andrew said, "that Henry's the one that made the issue clear for everyone when he showed that Englishmen can't be taxed except by men they've elected to represent them."

"That's right," Anderson agreed. "Henry's the one that made that plain ten years ago. He explained that so's people in the north as well as the south could understand it." The road dipped suddenly, and their horses splashed across a shallow ford. As they climbed the opposite bank, Anderson continued.

"That's the one issue that made sense to people in Virginia and people in New Jersey: no one has a right to take your money if you haven't elected them to do so in order to protect your society. And we Americans sure didn't elect anyone in the British Parliament! Henry made his famous speech in 1765, and they heard about it in all the colonies right away. That's when Americans in all the colonies knew that our ancient English rights were not going to be honored any longer by the British Parliament or by the King, unless we stood firm."

He paused for a while to collect his thoughts. They were walking their horses now to give them a breather. "All the colonies had legislatures elected by the people, and the King was supreme over all. That's how we've been governed. But when the King let Parliament overrule our legislatures, and steal our money by taxing us – which they'd no right to do – then Henry showed us that if we didn't stand against tyranny now, we'd all become slaves. He's the man that made all the colonies see what was at stake."

Andrew and Nathan followed Matthew Anderson up the steps and into the tavern, eager to meet the famous man. "Will they believe us?" Andrew asked his friend in a whisper as they waited to be let into the conference room.

"I sure hope so!" Nathan replied.

"Henry will!" Anderson said grimly. "I know it. Question is, will the others vote to support him? That's the question. He's called the Hanover Committee to meet, and he wants them to authorize the militia to march on Williamsburg. Let's pray that they'll vote to support him."

"Come on in," a militiaman said suddenly, opening the door for them. The man was tall, and he wore a long hunting shirt like the other militiamen. His belt also held a knife and toma-hawk. The boys followed Matthew Anderson into the room, and found themselves facing eight or nine men who were sitting around a table on which papers and letters were strewn. Several smoked their pipes, and they'd opened the windows to let in air. Nervously the two boys stood beside Anderson, one on either side of the grim woodsman.

"Matthew!" one of the men cried, jumping up and hurrying around the table to grip the woodsman's hand. Anderson introduced the two boys: "These are my friends, Patrick. They're the ones who kept Morgan from getting those letters."

"We heard about that!" Patrick Henry replied, shaking hands warmly with Andrew and Nathan.

He's over six feet tall! Andrew realized, as he studied the commanding presence of the man before him. Broad forehead, deep-set dark eyes, long face with a jutting jaw - *So this is Patrick Henry!*

Henry's eyes were penetrating but kind, Andrew noticed, and his voice the most pleasant he'd ever heard. Henry too wore a long hunting shirt, belted around the waist. His brown hair was short, his manner genial as he greeted them.

Returning to his seat, Henry sat down. Chairs were found for Anderson and the boys, and for almost thirty minutes the committee grilled the three about the news from Williamsburg. The men were visibly stirred about the fighting in Massachusetts.

Then they began to discuss the wisdom of continuing their march to confront the Governor at Williamsburg. Three of the men advised caution. "Let's wait," one said, "as some of the gentlemen in Williamsburg have advised us to do. They assure us that the Governor will return the powder if we need it.''

"We need it **now**!" George Dabney, Henry's cousin, said firmly. "You heard Matthew and those boys. Ebenezer Cuthburt just came from Massachusetts, where the British troops fired on the colonials who stood in their own town square, minding their own business! Then the soldiers marched to Concord and destroyed munitions and cannons that belonged to the Massachusetts people! They did it there, they'll do it here – if we let 'em! The British mean to subdue us! The Governor's already stolen our gunpowder! How can we wait any longer before we begin to defend ourselves?"

Several of the men murmured agreement. Patrick Henry spoke again. Andrew and Nathan were struck by the gentle tone with which he began. His voice was clear, with a country accent, they noted, but a down-to-earth form of expression, a naturalness that almost made them miss the power of his clear thought. He **pictured** things with words; he made them **see** and **feel** the tyranny they faced: the threatening power of the mighty British Empire, the looming slavery that approached them like the shadows at evening as the sun sank inexorably toward the western mountains. Listening to him, Andrew and Nathan could almost **feel** the chains being forged for them by the tyrannical British Government, almost **hear** their heavy clanking, and sense the hopelessness of coming enslavement. They shuddered.

The room was very quiet as Henry spoke. "This action of Governor Dunmore's is a fortunate circumstance for us," he asserted suddenly – to their complete surprise. "What he's done will rouse the people from the North to the South, from the coastal regions to the mountains. The farmers and the merchants, the woodsmen and the townspeople, the humblest honest poor and the most elegant aristocrat – all, all of them will understand this act as an act of tyranny!"

Leaning forward, his dark eyes burned into their souls as he spoke with awful solemnity. "Tell people about the British tax on tea, and those who prefer coffee will yawn – what's a tax on tea to them? But tell them the Governor's robbed their gunpowder from their Magazine, that he's stolen the means of defending our colony against Indians from the west, or against British soldiers from the sea; tell them that he's done this in concert with the British tyrants in Boston; **then** they'll realize that the end of their liberties has drawn near! **Then** they'll know that the noose of Parliamentary tyranny is drawing tight around their necks. Then they'll **feel** that rope – that rope with which England means to bind and enslave and hang them. **Then, then** they'll understand!" he cried.

Henry paused. Slowly his gaze moved from man to man around the table. When he spoke again, he spoke so softly that Andrew had to lean forward to hear him. "And gentlemen, when they **understand – they'll fight! I say it again - they'll fight!**"

His face is so grave, Andrew thought to himself. This patriot leader saw plainly what faced the colonies. He argued clearly, passionately, urging the committee to commit their men to march on Williamsburg to recover the stolen gunpowder.

Then Henry leaned back in his chair, and turned to the man on his right. "Mr. Chairman, let's allow these three men to retire. We must discuss this matter, and these messengers deserve a rest after their long ride from Williamsburg."

Matthew, Andrew, and Nathan realized at once that this was a polite way of dismissing them so the that committee could continue its discussion in private. They rose and turned to leave the room. Patrick Henry rose too, and came around the table to stand before them. Looking affectionately at Matthew Anderson, he grinned, raised his bushy eyebrows, and asked, "Matthew, so these are the two who laid that brute Zed unconscious on the floor and held a rifle on Morgan?"

"That's them, Patrick!" Matthew Anderson agreed.

"We learned about that from Johnson," Henry said, smiling at the astonishment on the boys' faces. "You know, the farmer you two stayed with after you left the tavern. He spread the word of your fight all over!"

Looking at the famous man, Andrew was struck by the kindness of his eyes. He began to understand how Henry had come to be loved by the common people. Henry spoke again, his face serious now.

"Andrew and Nathan, you struck a great blow for the cause of our freedom by keeping those letters from Morgan and the Governor! Virginia is in your debt!"

Flushing with pleasure at the gracious tribute, the two boys shook the firm hand Henry offered them.

He continued. "I learned from the Williamsburg committee that it was your two sisters who heard that the Governor planned to arrest me. Would you please thank them for the brave way in which they got this information, and passed it on? This was a surprise, frankly – I didn't think the Governor would do this, and had taken no thought to protect myself from him.

Now I have. Please tell the girls this. And tell them that the next time I come to Williamsburg, I want to meet them and thank them personally." His grave face broke into a smile.

"Yes, sir," the boys said. "Thank you sir." They turned and followed Matthew Anderson from the room.

Chapter Sixteen

THE MARCH ON WILLIAMSBURG!

Later that afternoon, Matthew Anderson and the two boys came out of the tavern after downing a huge meal, and joined a group of the local militia who were lounging under a big oak, waiting for orders from the committee.

"Have you heard what they've decided?" asked a huge militiaman as he leaned on his long rifle. A band of cloth slanted across his broad chest and on this were written the words, "Liberty Or Death," which was a quote from Patrick Henry's famous speech. Many of the other militiamen wore these bands also.

"No, we haven't," Matthew Anderson replied. "We've been eating in the big room. They're still meeting in the back."

"Well, we're ready to go whenever Mr. Henry tells us," the man said grimly. "Those men from Williamsburg that rode through here yesterday on their way to Philadelphia, they tried to persuade us to trust the Governor, disband and go home. But we won't do it. We don't trust the Governor any more than Mr. Henry does."

Just then a crowd of men poured out of the tavern from behind them. It was the committee! One of them called across the road to the sergeant, yelling for him to assemble the militia. Shouts filled the air as the eager armed men rushed to stand before the tavern. A drum called other units to assemble. With hearts pounding, Andrew and Nathan followed Anderson across the road and joined the jostling crowd of armed men. Then Patrick Henry stepped forward.

Instantly the men broke into cheers. Solemn faced, he waved them to silence, and thanked them. Then he explained the committee's decision. "Our liberties are at stake, men!" he cried. "Our homes are in danger. The blessed prosperity which the good God has given this colony is threatened by the hand of a tyrannical government."

Henry paused, and the men muttered angrily. "What can we do, Mr. Henry?" called out a man from the back of the formation.

"We can do a lot! Because we can't let evil men in government take away our liberties and harm our families! We can't let wicked men steal our means of defending our homes! We can't let our friends who refuse to see this danger paralyze our resolve by persuading us to lie prostrate under the tyrant's boots! And men, we fight not only for ourselves. We fight for liberty and for justice. And I have no doubt that the same God Whose power divided the Red Sea for the deliverance of Israel still rules in all His glory, unchanged and unchangeable! He it is Who has hardened the Governor's heart by allowing him to commit the outrageous theft of our Colony's gunpowder, as He hardened the heart of Pharaoh and allowed that tyrant to afflict His chosen people in Egypt. It is now up to us to prove that we are worthy of this Divine interference on our behalf. We've got to march! We've got to recover the gunpowder our taxes paid for, or make the Governor pay us for its replacement!

We've got to show the British that Virginians cannot be en-slaved! Will you march with me to Williamsburg?"

Roars of approval greeted his appeal. Cheers rent the air. The men were thrilled that they had such a leader, and it was with difficulty that they were quieted. Orders were given, the company assembled, and, with Patrick Henry and several officers at their head, the men marched out of town.

Henry called a halt when the column reached Park's Spring. "We'll camp here, men," he cried. The men broke ranks at once and began to set up camp. Cooking fires were lit, and soon the militia were eating their suppers.

"Follow me, boys," Matthew Andrew said quietly to An-drew and Nathan. "I've got a friend who owns the farm just down the road. We'll sleep in his barn."

The boys rode with the woodsman to the home of his friend. Here they put their horses in the barn, unsaddled, and rubbed the tired animals down. Then they trooped to the house to enjoy a meal with the family in their kitchen. After eating, they returned to the barn, broke out their blankets, and climbed the ladder to the loft. Here they spread their blankets in the deep straw, and soon were fast asleep.

Andrew thought he'd just closed his eyes when he felt Matthew Anderson's hand shaking his shoulder. "Time to get up, boys!" the woodsman said with a grin. "You plannin' on sleepin' while Patrick Henry leads us to Williamsburg?"

That brought both boys to their feet at once. "What do you think the Governor will do, Mr. Anderson?" Nathan asked, as they gathered their packs and weapons. "Will he fight us?"

"He'll be hopelessly outnumbered if he does," Anderson replied. "Not that our group is that large – it's not. But the other counties are sending militia too. If the Governor starts a shooting war, he'll be surrounded; he'll never escape to the British ships in the river. I don't think he'll fight. But you never know. He's proud. He's hot-headed. And he's used to power. Men who are used to power don't like to be checked by anyone. They can do stupid things sometimes. Don't ever forget that!"

The three rode to the militia camp, and ate a quick breakfast with a group of Anderson's friends. Then they reported to Henry, who was standing in the midst of his aides.

"Matthew," Henry said, as the three approached, "we'll get more messengers from Williamsburg today. Ride ahead of our formation, and screen them for me. If you think they're suspicious, stop them and send one of these young men back to warn us. If they seem legitimate, have one of the boys escort them back to me. We'll keep the others with us when they arrive," he said with a grin, "so they can't ride back and tell the Governor the size of our force!"

"Fine, Patrick," Anderson replied. "Let's ride, boys."

The three mounted and galloped down the road to get a headstart on the marching men who would follow them. Behind them, the militia companies formed, drums and fifes began a lively tune, and the column swung vigorously into movement. Patrick Henry and his officers were mounted, and rode ahead of the marching column. Someone called for a tune, and the men quickened their pace and broke into rousing song.

Throughout the morning, Henry sent out scouts and messengers. Several times, Matthew Anderson and the boys stopped single riders from Williamsburg. Twice these men claimed to have messages from the Governor for Patrick Henry. Each time, Matthew sent them back with one of the boys to deliver their report.

Around nine in the morning, Andrew escorted a small man in red uniform atop a huge black horse back to Patrick Henry. Henry read the man's message, then turned to Captain Meredith. "This man's from the Governor, Captain. The Governor's demanding we halt, return to our counties, and disperse."

Smiling thinly, Captain Samuel Meredith replied: "Impossible!"

"It is impossible!" Henry agreed. "Let this man march with us, Captain. We wouldn't want him to ride to Williamsburg ahead of us, would we!"

"No, Patrick, we wouldn't!" Meredith agreed, calling a man to take the reins of the messenger's horse while ordering the rider to dismount. The Governor's messenger frowned helplessly; he'd been ordered to return with news about the size of Henry's force. Now he was a prisoner! Scowling with anger, he joined the column of marching men. The militiamen laughed, called for another tune, and struck up another spirited song about liberty.

Around noon, the group passed through the New Kent Court House, and learned that that county too was calling its citizens to arms. The militiamen cheered this news and the column quickened its pace. In early afternoon they crossed the causeway across the swampy ground near Riffin's Ferry, followed the river for a while, then came out onto the high road that led to the capital.

Later, a messenger from the patriots in Williamsburg galloped toward Matthew Anderson and the two boys. Recognizing the man, Matthew Anderson waved him on without halting. "Must have some urgent news!" he speculated, as the rider waved back and raced past.

Half-an-hour later the three had just crossed a stream when they heard hoof beats behind. Turning, they saw one of Patrick Henry's aides galloping to overtake them.

"Hold up," Anderson said, pulling his horse to a stop, turning to meet the fast-riding man; "that's Ben Coleman.'" Nathan and Andrew halted their mounts, and turned to face the rider.

"Henry says to keep a sharp look-out," Coleman said as he pulled up to the three. "That last messenger from Williamsburg told us that the Governor's given muskets to Indians and servants, rolled out cannons on the Palace Green, and threatened to blow up the houses in town if Patrick Henry doesn't turn this column around. He's also brought British marines from the ships. So keep your eyes open, and be ready to tell us at once if you spot hostile forces."

"We'll do that," Matthew Anderson said. "But cannons on the Palace Green? That's crazy! With all the militia companies marching to Williamsburg? He's hopelessly outnumbered."

"He is," Coleman replied. A stocky man on a huge brown horse, Coleman looked worried. "But some of the companies we expected to join us have turned back."

"Turned back!" Anderson exclaimed. "Why?"

"Some of the leaders in the House of Burgesses persuaded them to go home and trust the Governor to return the gunpowder if we really need it."

Anderson and the boys were appalled at this news.

Coleman continued. "Now we're worried that the Virginians will be divided – and that a lot of them will want to let the Governor get away with stealing our powder! We don't know how many of the counties will support us."

"What!" Anderson replied, shocked. "After all we've learned about the war up north?"

"Yep," the man replied. "But some are saying we Virginians shouldn't go to war just because of some hotheads in Massachusetts. So they went home."

Andrew and Nathan looked at each other soberly. What would happen, they wondered? Ben Coleman pulled his horse around and galloped back to the column. Worried now, Anderson and the boys resumed their ride, and soon arrived at a tavern and store called Duncastle's Ordinary. They passed this and kept going.

It wasn't long before messengers began riding up from behind them, heading toward Williamsburg. The three waved at the men as they galloped past. "Henry's trying to find out what's going on in the town," Anderson speculated.

Behind them, the marching column crossed the causeway below Ruffin's Ferry, just as Matthew and the boys had done earlier, and came out on the high road that led to the capital. In late afternoon the militia finally reached the popular tavern called Duncastle's Ordinary, and Henry ordered a halt.

"We'll rest here a while, men!" he called. Scouts were sent out in all directions, and guards posted. The rest of the men spread out in the yard and began to cook their rations.

Chapter Seventeen

THE GOVERNOR'S CANNONS

Frantic confusion dominated the broad green in front of the Governor's Palace in Williamsburg. Groups of red-coated marines rushed about, warning the crowd of curious civilians to move away. Other soldiers wrestled wheeled cannons through the broad gate of the high brick wall surrounding the Palace, and moved these to face down the green, a long grassed area bordered by trees and flanked by houses across the streets. A group of Indians and servants, with muskets in their hands, moved in a dazed way as a red-coated soldier yelled at them and tried to show them how to line up in proper formation.

Servants throughout the large brick Palace were barricading windows and doors, making a tremendous clatter. Guards in the back garden watched against a sudden patriot assault from the woods to the north of the long wall that surrounded the Palace. Other guards were spread thinly along the wall, and at the various buildings that dotted the enclosed yard surrounding the Governor's mansion. Urgent shouts filled the air as stewards called for food and supplies to be brought from the smaller out-buildings into the Palace. It was obvious to the watching citizens that the Governor had ordered his servants to stock up the Palace for a possible siege.

A red-coated marine on a sweat-streaked black horse gal-loped down the green toward the front gate of the Palace. Pulling up before the guard in a swirling cloud of dust, the man leaped from the saddle with practiced ease, threw the reins to the soldier, and rushed inside, calling for the sergeant of the guard. He was taken at once to the Governor in his office.

Inside the marvelously paneled room with its high windows and rich furnishings, the Governor of the Colony of Virginia was in a towering rage. Flanked by two red-coated officers, he stood beside his desk, trying to decipher the latest reports his galloping scouts kept bringing him. When this newest messen-ger told him that Patrick Henry's militia had reached Dun-castle's Ordinary, the Governor's large red face became even redder.

"Duncastle's Ordinary!" the Governor stormed, veins swel-ling in his powerful neck, eyes bulging with fury. "Patrick Henry's at Duncastle's Ordinary! That's only fifteen miles from here!"

"Yes, sir," the marine quailed before the enraged Governor.

"How many men does he have with him?" the captain of marines asked the scout.

"We don't know, sir," the man replied. "The messengers you sent don't return; we think Henry's keeping them so they can't tell us anything!"

"We don't know?" the Governor stormed. He pounded his thick fist on the desk. "We've **got** to know!"

"Yes, sir," the man said, quailing before the Governor's violent rage. "We've tried, sir. But we can't get through their scouts. They've got companies all around town now, and our men can't get through."

"Then we'll blow the town down with our cannons!" the Governor shouted, turning to the captain of the marines. "We'll level them all, Captain!"

"Well, sir," the officer said hesitantly, awed at the enormity of the crime against the townspeople that his superior was proposing. "But we don't want to hurt civilians, sir. And they haven't shot at us yet."

"Haven't shot at us yet?" Governor Dunmore yelled. "Haven't shot at us yet? Does an armed mob surrounding the King's Governor have to shoot to be in rebellion?"

"No, sir," the captain said, "but..."

"Governor," a quiet voice interjected. Governor Dunmore turned and looked at the speaker, a slender lieutenant of infantry who'd been visiting the Governor when the crisis erupted.

"The captain's right, sir," the lieutenant continued smoothly. "We don't yet have reason to fire - certainly not at the people's homes. And the countryside is filled with these armed militia companies. We're completely surrounded."

"You're afraid of that rabble?" the Governor shouted, outraged, eyes bulging, arms waving. "Do you think they can stand against British marines?"

He looked as if he were about to explode. The lieutenant took a deep breath. "No, sir, the colonial militia can't stand against our soldiers and marines. Not ordinarily. But there are very few marines with us now, sir." He spoke slowly, calmly

— as if to a frantic child. They **had** to make the Governor see reason!

"And there are hundreds and hundreds of their militia in this part of the state, Governor," the marine officer added. "Every county's got its own force."

"But the Virginia leaders themselves persuaded many of that rabble to disperse and go home!" the Governor remonstrated hotly. "They don't have all their force by any means. British regulars will scatter those remaining undisciplined militia like straw in a strong wind!"

"True, sir," the officer of marines replied, "but right now they have many more men than we do here. And they're between us and the ships. We'd never fight our way through to the river if shooting started, not with all the women and children and servants we've got. And your family, Governor — we don't want to endanger them."

Suddenly, the Governor stopped his frenzied motions, and looked intently at the two officers. "You're saying it's a precarious situation militarily?" Dunmore asked, quieter now.

"That's exactly it, sir!" the lieutenant of infantry replied. "For us, here, cut off from the ships, with so few fighting men, it **is** a precarious situation militarily. When we get some of the regiments the King is sending to the colonies, we'll be in a completely different situation. But we don't have those regiments yet."

"Then we've got to bide our time?" the Governor asked. His shoulders slumped as he turned to the window. But he was listening to reason now, his officers realized; they began to breathe more easily.

"I think we do for now, Governor," the marine officer said. "At least for now."

"But Henry's demanding that I give him back that gunpowder," the Governor said, raising his voice again and turning to face them. "I'll fight before I give him back one barrel!"

"Well, sir," the lieutenant of infantry replied soothingly, "he's now asking that we give him a check for the value of the powder. We've got the powder, and he knows it."

"He's offering a compromise, Governor," the marine officer interjected. "His last message demanded either the powder or a valid check for its full value. He's willing to compromise."

But the word 'compromise' enraged the Governor once more. "Compromise with a rebel?" he shouted. "Compromise with a rebel?" he repeated, louder now, face red, neck muscles bulging again, thick fist pounding the table once more. "I'd rather blow the town down and die fighting!"

Several blocks away from the Palace, Nelson Edwards had brought his family to William Hendricks' home. "With the boys gone," William had told his friend, "we could defend our families easier from one house than from two, Nelson." Edwards had agreed, and now his wife was working with the Hendricks to ready the house for whatever dangers they might face. Sarah and Rachel were playing with the two younger Edwards boys to keep them from worrying about all the activity.

They had plenty of food in the storeroom below the house, plenty of water in barrels, and their weapons were loaded. Hendricks and Edwards finally decided that they'd done all they could to prepare for the worst. The two men wandered out onto the front porch of the house and searched the street. It seemed safe enough, they saw, with civilians walking along periodically. Other families were similarly preparing, and occasional riders galloped along the road, waving as they passed.

No British soldiers were near; the Governor's forces were all concentrated at the Palace.

"At least we've got armed neighbors," Hendricks observed. "We don't have to defend our families alone."

"Thank the Lord for that!" Nelson agreed. "But heaven protect those families near the Palace if the Governor does what he's threatened and turns his cannons on the town!"

"It'd be terrible!" William agreed. "But the British have destroyed homes in New England before. And after they shot our militia at Lexington, they burned down homes on their retreat to Boston. They even burned houses where no patriot snipers had shot at them. They wrecked and plundered all the way home!"

"Worse still," Nelson replied grimly, "back in 1757, they forced families in Albany, New York, to take in seventeen hundred common soldiers – into their homes to live! – because they didn't want to pay for barracks. Can you imagine those dregs from prisons and slums living with our wives and daughters?"

"They couldn't do that if the temper of their nation was sound," Nelson replied. "But when the people as a whole have no sense of God, the leaders will be no better. Evil government is usually a sign of God's judgment against an evil people."

Suddenly a rider galloped up, tossed a package at their feet, and raced down the street. "Thanks!" Hendricks yelled, picking up the package and tearing it open.

"It's from the committee," he read. "Henry and a column of militia are at Duncastle's Ordinary, fifteen miles away. The Governor has threatened to destroy the town if he comes any closer. Henry is demanding a receipt – on a valid London bank – for the full value of the gunpowder the Governor stole, plus money to pay for its shipment here. Pray and keep your guns ready!"

"Well," Nelson Edwards said thoughtfully, "that threat to blow down the houses with his cannons is a bluff. The minute they fired on peoples' homes, our riflemen would shoot down every cannoneer in sight. Those guns won't do him a bit of good in such close quarters because he can't keep us from shooting the men behind them."

"You're right, Nelson. But it's a nasty threat just the same. It shows what kind of tyranny we're facing that he'd even make such a statement." He turned toward the door and called for his daughter.

"Laura!" She came out, and he handed her the package. "Take this across the street, please, and give it to the Davises. Then come right back."

"Yes, Father," she smiled, hazel eyes wide with curiosity as she took the package from her father and stepped off the front porch. The sun shone on the reddish-brown hair of the girl as she crossed the street.

Nelson Edwards turned to his friend and smiled. "Your Laura is a lovely and virtuous young woman, William. Are you going to let young Clark court her, as he's asked?"

"Yes, I am." Hendricks replied with a smile. "He's a godly man, Nelson – the kind of man we've prayed for. He's honorable. He's disciplined. He knows how to work and how to save. And his family's as fine as we could wish."

He paused, then added, "He's also been beating me in chess! I've got to keep him coming over here so I can even the score!"

Both men laughed at this. Then Hendricks looked at his friend with a smile: "Funny thing. When our girls are little, we don't think the time will come when we'll have to give them up, do we!"

"No, not really!" Nelson laughed. "But that's why we raise them."

"It is indeed!" Hendricks agreed. His face grew more solemn. "And that's why we've got to defend them from harm, so they'll live long enough to have their own families, and raise their own godly children."

"I'll be glad when Nathan and Andrew return," Nelson said quietly.

"Speaking of those boys," Hendricks said with a smile, "you'd better be thinking about the future yourself! My son can't seem to stay away from your Sarah's pies! Or her deep blue eyes!"

Nelson Edwards threw back his head and laughed out loud. "My pies, you mean! Sometimes she gives them to him before I can get a bite!" Then he grew serious. "I think about it a lot, William, and it pleases me no end! Of course, they're young yet. But, Mary and I hope things keep going the way they are now."

"So do we." Hendricks said quietly.

A rider galloped down the street and hauled up before them in a storm of dust. "The committee wants everyone ready for war!" he cried. "We don't know if the Governor will fire on the town or not!" He rushed off to shout the message to other homes.

Grim-faced, Hendricks called across the street for Laura to come home. "All right, Father," she called back, as she stepped off the Davis' porch and hurried home.

"Let's get the families together and pray, Nelson," Hendricks said quietly. "Things look bad."

Chapter Eighteen

"THE DRUMS OF WAR!"

Things looked bad to Patrick Henry and his officers as they stood under a large oak beside Duncastle's Ordinary and discussed the latest dispatch the messenger had just brought from Williamsburg.

Captain Meredith reminded them of its content. "The Governor's got his cannons in front of the Palace, trained on the homes of citizens. He's swearing that if we cross the river and head for Williamsburg, he'll blow down all the houses within range of the guns!"

Captain Meredith looked up from the letter and laughed. "That'd be the stupidest thing he could do! Our men would pick off those soldiers at the cannons before they could reload. The redcoats would have to retreat behind those walls, and then we'd get those guns during the night!"

"It's just a threat to scare the people," Parker Goodall said. "A nasty threat."

Captain Meredith continued reading. "Another messenger says the British warship off Yorktown has its guns trained on that town too. When the Governor sends the word, the ship's cannons will demolish all the houses it can hit!"

"That's a real threat," he added, looking up from the letter. "There's nothing our riflemen in Yorktown could do to stop those ships' guns from destroying all the homes within their range."

"But there's a lot our militia could do to starve out the Governor here in Williamsburg, or take the Palace by storm, if he ordered such a dreadful deed!" Henry said grimly. "Governor Dunmore had better not forget that he's surrounded, and could never fight his way to the British ships through our militia."

"The Governor's got more marines within the walls of his Palace in Williamsburg, Patrick," the messenger told him. "He says he means to fight if we march any closer."

"Did you tell him we **will** march to Williamsburg if he doesn't pay for the powder he stole?" the grim faced Henry replied.

"We sure did, Patrick, but the Governor's in a towering rage. Says his honor's at stake; says he can't negotiate under threat from rebels. That's what he calls us, 'rebels'!"

"Another militia company's going home," Captain Meredith said grimly. "They've been persuaded we shouldn't confront the Governor."

"Some of our leaders have already left for the Continental Congress," Parker Goodall said, "I'd hoped that they'd stay with us and help us get our gunpowder back!" Young Goodall was one of Henry's closest friends, and this news grieved him; would they all flee and leave Henry alone to fight for their liberty?

"Some of our Virginia leaders are afraid, I think," Patrick Henry said quietly. "Even men of principle are hesitating now. It's as if they've walked to the edge of a river bank, and are afraid to take the long step required to reach the other side! But it's **Liberty** that's on the other side," he cried, "and it's **Slavery** if they don't cross over!"

There was a murmur of fervent assent to this. These men had followed Patrick Henry because they believed that he was right. Honest men had to take a stand somewhere to defend their liberties from the tyranny of all-powerful government, they reasoned, or else they, and their families, would become slaves.

But many men in Virginia, and in the other colonies, were wavering.

Patrick Henry had never wavered. He didn't believe for a minute the Governor's promise that he'd return the powder if it were needed. He did not accept the arguments of those who advised Virginians to hope for a peaceful solution with Great Britain. He knew that the English Parliament would never restore the accustomed liberties of the American colonies. English armies were already afloat, escorted by the all-powerful British navy, sailing for the American shores. Henry was certain that the British regiments in the northern colonies would never leave until Parliament's rule was supreme and unchallenged. And he knew that England meant to subdue Virginia just as she meant to subdue Massachusetts, and was sending armies and navies to achieve that end.

Patrick Henry never wavered in his resolve because he refused to indulge in wishful hopes. He'd seen the principle upon which all these mighty movements of Parliament's fleets and armies moved – the principle of domination.

"Who shall rule us, sirs?" he'd cried again and again in the meetings of the House of Burgesses. "That is the issue before us now: Who shall rule us? Shall it be men we have chosen, men who know our circumstances, men who share our situation and understand our capabilities? Or shall it be men whose souls have been bought by powerful factions, men who live far away and are unresponsive to our needs and hopes, men who care nothing for our problems but who care everything for the wishes – and the pressures – of those groups to whom they've sold their votes and their souls?"

If the issues seemed clouded to many honest Virginians, they were not clouded to Patrick Henry. "The war has already begun!" he'd cried in the meeting of the House of Burgesses. "The next gale that sweeps from the north will bring to our ears the clash of resounding arms! Our brethren in the north are already in the field! Why stand we here idle?"

Again and again he'd warned the Virginia legislators that the English government that ruled over them was no longer representative of them. "Those men in Parliament care nothing for our colony;" he cried, "they care everything for the hand that feeds them and keeps them in office! The noose is tightening around our necks! We must fight if our families are to be freed of this tyranny! I repeat it, sirs, we must fight!" And over the years, Henry had persuaded many men that one day they must indeed be ready to fight if they wished to remain free.

Throughout the afternoon the militia encampment at Duncastle's Ordinary had been the scene of vigorous activity. Messengers galloped in and out through the assembled soldiers, seeking Patrick Henry. He'd sent men to warn the patriots at Yorktown to guard against Governor Dunmore's escaping through their port. He'd warned the militia leaders in other Virginia counties about possible British movements. He'd learned that more militia companies had listened to the voice of those who'd advised them to disperse and return home.

"How many men have we got, Patrick?" Captain Meredith asked, reading the latest report. "Who will stand with us now? Have they all lost their courage? Don't they know that if we stand together we can stand against the Governor? But if we dissolve like this, we'll be destroyed one by one?" The honest man was angered at this breach in the ranks of the patriots.

"How many men have we got?" Henry asked, eyes flashing, voice rising. "We've got enough! That's how many we've got! Others are marching to join us! We know the majority of the people are with us. Those militia companies that dispersed will return if we need 'em. It only takes a few determined men to change the course of history. We've got those determined men with us! They know what's at stake. They'll fight to protect their homes and their liberty!"

But for several hours the issue appeared to hang in the balance. Late that afternoon a messenger from the Treasurer of the Colony galloped in from Williamsburg, bearing a ckeck for three hundred and thirty pounds of English money to pay for the powder the Governor had taken from the Magazine. Matthew Anderson and the boys escorted him to the camp, and led him to Patrick Henry. The patriot leader was standing under a large oak conferring with two of his officers.

"Here's a man from the Treasurer in Williamsburg, Patrick," Anderson said. "He says he's got money to pay for the powder. The Governor has agreed to pay us back."

The officers around Henry broke into smiles. "You've made him give in, Patrick!" one said.

But to everyone's surprise, Henry refused to accepted the money offered by the messenger. He distrusted the receipts, he said, and explained to his officers that the Governor might refuse to honor them should he flee the Colony for England.

"We've got to have receipts which will be accepted whether or not the Governor remains in Virginia," he said, "receipts from a good London bank, one we can trust. Go back and tell the Governor that!" Henry commanded, staring at the shocked messenger.

Shaken by Henry's refusal, the man mounted his horse, turned, and headed for Williamsburg. "Let's rest for the night," Henry said to his officers then. "Have the men make camp. Tomorrow we march – unless the Governor pays us with money we can trust."

Orders were given, and the men who couldn't pack into the inn rolled up in their blankets in the large yard. Matthew Anderson, in his typical fashion, had wrangled a spot for himself, Andrew and Nathan in a shed behind the inn. They tethered their horses in the barn, ate supper with a group of the militiamen, then went to the small shed, rolled up in their blankets, and fell fast asleep.

The troop was awake at dawn. The men ate a quick breakfast, and prepared to march. Messengers came in with news from the capital, however, and no orders for marching were given. As the men waited for orders, they debated among themselves the issues before them. Did they really have enough men to force the British Governor to return their powder, or to pay for its replacement? Would enough militia join them to make Governor Dunmore give in? While the Governor armed his servants and slaves, the English soldiers and marines from the warships in the York River augmented Governor Dunmore's own forces. While the families in Williamsburg barricaded their doors and waited with rifles loaded for the Governor's cannons to fire, the patriots with Patrick Henry braced themselves to march on Williamsburg if the Governor failed to give in.

The morning was still young when several men galloped in on sweat-streaked horses through the patriot lines and hauled to a stop in a swirl of dust before Henry and his officers. Leaping from the saddle, they dismounted. With great respect Henry saluted the honored Thomas Nelson, Jr., a prominent merchant of Yorktown, and introduced him and his companion to his officers. Gravely Mr. Nelson explained the bank draft he handed to Patrick Henry.

"That's a check for three hundred and thirty pounds of English money, Mr. Henry," he said, "drawn, you will recognize, on a good London bank. I will personally guarantee payment of this money."

"Then we need no other assurance, Mr. Nelson," Henry said respectfully. "You have done Virginia – and our liberties – a great service, sir."

Henry's solemn face broke into a broad smile. Handing the letter and the check to Captain Meredith, he stepped away from his officers and approached the marshaled ranks of armed men. His eyes were shining as he cried out in his ringing voice, "The Governor will pay for the powder!"

"They finally listened, Patrick!" Captain Meredith said, with a broad grin. "The Governor's given in! You've won!"

"**We've** won!" Henry corrected, spreading out his arms to indicate all the men who'd marched with them. "Virginia has won!"

The militiamen ran toward Henry and began to cheer wildly, tossing their caps in the air, firing their muskets. They made a tremendous din, and other groups rushed over to hear the news. Then they too joined in celebrating the patriot victory. Again and again they cheered the man who'd won this bloodless battle for the colony – Patrick Henry. Again and again they fired their muskets, reloaded and fired again. The drums began to beat a thrilling staccato march, and the yelling grew louder.

Henry grinned and grinned at their cheers, then waved his arms for quiet. He waved and waved, but the men would not stop cheering. Finally, the noise lessened; gradually the celebrating men stopped their shouting; at last a hush fell over the crowd of armed men.

"The Governor's going to pay with a check drawn on a bank we can trust!" Henry said, eyes flashing. "And he's going to pay for transporting the powder to Virginia, too!"

The men began to cheer again. "You've done it, Patrick!" a rifleman shouted, "You've done it! All the others said we shouldn't anger the Governor by protesting what he'd done. But you've made him pay for what he stole!" Yells and shouts filled the air again. The drummers began to beat their drums in a lively cadence, and the fifes joined in. Again and again the men cheered Henry.

For them the picture was very clear: one man had the courage to stand up to the tyrannical act of their government. One man had stood fast – while others had wavered, or dodged a confrontation. One man had rallied them for the march to Williamsburg. And one man had forced the British Governor to pay for the powder he had stolen from the Americans. That man was Patrick Henry. The men cheered that man.

Several hours later, Matthew Anderson parted from Andrew and Nathan. "We're sending a military escort with Patrick Henry," he explained, "so the Governor can't arrest him on his way to the Continental Congress. We can't let the British capture him now! They'd take him to England and hang him for sure. So we're escorting him to Maryland. Crowds of militia are waiting for him there! He'll go to the Continental Congress like a victorious general returning from winning a war!"

"That's just what he is!" Andrew said proudly.

"That's exactly what he is!" Anderson agreed with a grin.

Just then another company of militia marched down the road to the tune of fifes and drums. Anderson looked thoughtfully at them as they approached. "Hear those drums, boys?" he asked.

They said that they did.

"Hear them well. Those are the drums of war. It's already begun. There's no turning back now, not 'til it's over." He waved and walked toward his mount.

As Andrew and Nathan turned to leave, Patrick Henry hurried over. His usually serious face broke into a kindly smile.

"Thank you again, men!" he said. "And thank your sisters for discovering the Governor's plans to arrest me! Because of that news, the militia are going with me to the Maryland shore. Tell those brave girls I am deeply grateful for what they've done!" He shook their hands warmly, then turned and waved to the troops, who cheered wildly. Running to his mount Henry leaped into the saddle and galloped off amid a crowd of mounted escorts.

Chapter Nineteen

THE HOMECOMING

Dark was falling as Andrew and Nathan approached the town of Williamsburg. Both boys were stiff and sore from their four days in the saddle. "Gosh, I'm tired, Nathan!" Andrew said, shifting his weight.

"So am I!" Nathan replied. "I don't know whether it's all the riding these past four days, or all the worrying about whether or not we'd have a war in our town, but it's worn me to a frazzle!"

They passed a company of marching men who were roaring out the words of a stirring song about liberty to the cadence beat by three drummer boys at the head of the column.

"Liberty or death!" the company commander yelled as the boys rode up. "Liberty or death!" seventy men roared out in unison.

"Liberty or death!" the two boys shouted back, waving their hats at the marching men who were heading home.

"Gosh, Andrew," Nathan exclaimed, eyes shining, "we're not alone, and neither is Patrick Henry! There are a lot of folks who'll fight for liberty!"

Only later did the boys and their fathers learn that more than five thousand Virginia militia were marching rapidly to join Patrick Henry at Williamsburg. And that thousands more were mobilizing in the western counties. While some of their leaders had hesitated, the majority of Virginians had not.

Darkness was falling as the boys rode up to Nathan's house, dismounted stiffly, and tied the horses to the rail. They were so tired now that they stumbled as they turned and headed toward the steps. Suddenly the door of the house burst open, light flooded the porch, and their sisters rushed toward the tired travelers. Laura and Rachel threw their arms around Andrew, nearly knocking him down, while Sarah hugged her big brother and cried with joy. Then their mothers and fathers and the smaller children rushed down the steps, and everyone was talking at once.

Like heroes home from victorious war, the two boys were led back into the Edwards' home. Candles were lit in the rooms against the growing darkness, plates were set on the long table in the dining room, mugs filled with cool cider were put beside the plates, and from the kitchen came the most wonderful smells!

"I made a pie, Andrew!" Sarah whispered to him as they crowded through the door into the room.

"And I've got muffins waiting at home!" Rachel smiled, hugging him again and again.

"Wait a minute!" Nathan protested to the shining-eyed girl, as he followed a step behind. "What about me? I'm starvin'!"

Rachel laughed. "Oh, maybe there's one for you."

"Let the boys wash up!" Mrs. Edwards cried. "My goodness, girls! There's more dirt on these two than there is on the road! Give them a minute to get clean!"

The two fathers stood outside the crowd that almost crushed their two sons, smiling proudly. They'd taken the boys' rifles as they'd entered, and stacked them against the wall.

As the boys went to wash, Nelson said quietly to his friend, "They didn't need their guns this time, thank the Lord!"

"Not this time!" William Hendricks agreed. "And neither did we!"

"It was close, William."

"Very close. The man I spoke with just before the boys got back said that Henry and his men were about to march. The Governor gave in just in time!"

"Henry **had** to march, if the Governor hadn't given in! There was no other way. There comes a time when you've got to draw a line, and defend what's on your side of that line."

"Like our families, our property and our liberty," William Hendricks replied soberly.

Then the girls were calling out and crowding around as Andrew and Nathan returned, hands and faces hastily cleaned, tired faces beaming with new life. The laughing mothers called for their husbands to join the family in the dining room, and with hearts full of gratitude, the two fathers went to the table. Men and boys held chairs for the ladies and girls, then sat down themselves.

Before they ate, Nelson Edwards opened the family Bible and began to read the ninety-fifth Psalm.

"O come, let us sing unto the Lord: let us make a joyful noise to the rock of our salvation.

Let us come before His presence with thanksgiving, and make a joyful noise unto Him with psalms.

For the Lord is a great God, and a great King above all gods."

With tears of gratitude in his eyes, Nelson Edwards closed the Bible and looked around at his family and his closest friends. "Let's thank the Lord, before we eat." He led the joyful group in prayer.

MASSACHUSETTS

April - June 1775

In Massachusetts British troops marched on to Lexington,

To seize the Patriot Leaders, and wreck their Stores and
Guns;

But Paul Revere rode desperately to warn the Towns and
Farms,

And soon the night was shattered by the sound of the Alarms

That rang from church bells, Town to Town, and through
the Countryside,

And woke the sleeping Citizens and brought Men, side by
side,

In marching ranks to Lexington, where there they saw the
Slain –

The Patriots the British troops shot on their Village Green.

Militiamen from other towns formed ranks and hurried
round,

They struck the dreaded Redcoats as they left the blood-
stained Ground;

They shot them as they fled the fateful Field of Lexington,

They chased them back to Boston and the shelter of its
Guns.

And then the Patriots formed a Guard round Boston, and its
Bay,
And bottled up the Tyrants in the Town wherein they lay.
But when the British troops attacked – to break our Peoples'
Will –
They lost a thousand Redcoats on the slopes 'round Bunker
Hill.

The Providence Foundation

The Providence Foundation offers other books and videos that may be of interest to you. The book *America's Providential History* examines how God guided our nation from the very beginning and how America grew from Christian principles. *The Story of America's Liberty* is a 60-minute video highlighting the Christian history of America, including many providential occurrences during our founding.

The Foundation also provides speakers on America's Christian history and many other topics. For more information or a free catalog and order blank of our books, tapes, and materials contact: The Providence Foundation, P.O. Box 6759, Charlottesville, VA 22906. Phone/Fax: 804-978-4535. E-mail: provfdn@aol.com

The Providence Foundation is a non-profit, Christian educational organization whose mission is to assist in spreading liberty, justice, and prosperity among the nations by teaching and equipping people in a Biblical philosophy of life. Emphasis is upon educating in principles, rather than issues, drawing upon examples in history for illustration. The history of early America is especially emphasized since the religious, social, educational, and political life of the nation at that time was primarily shaped by the Bible.

Be on the look out for other books in the series to follow *Drums of War.*